Black Earth

OrangeBooks Publication

Smriti Nagar, Bhilai, Chhattisgarh - 490020

Website: **www.orangebooks.in**

© Copyright, 2023, Author

All rights reserved. No part of this book may be reproduced, stored in a retrieval system, or transmitted, in any form by any means, electronic, mechanical, magnetic, optical, chemical, manual, photocopying, recording or otherwise, without the prior written consent of its writer.

First Edition, 2023
ISBN: 978-93-5621-647-1

BLACK EARTH

Dr. Spinder Kour

OrangeBooks Publication
www.orangebooks.in

INDEX

Chapter 1 1

Chapter 2 5

Chapter 3 12

Chapter 4 17

Chapter 5 24

Chapter 6 29

Chapter 7 32

Chapter 8 37

Chapter 9 42

Chapter 10 49

Chapter 11 53

Chapter 12 57

Chapter 13 61

Chapter 14 64

Chapter 15 68

Chapter 16	71
Chapter 17	76
Chapter 18	82
Chapter 19	88
Chapter 20	92
Chapter 21	96
Chapter 22	102
Chapter 23	105
Chapter 24	111
Chapter 25	115
Chapter 26	118
Chapter 27	121
Chapter 28	125
Chapter 29	130
Chapter 30	134
Chapter 31	137
Chapter 32	141
Chapter 33	148
Chapter 34	154
Chapter 35	158

Chapter 36 162

Chapter 37 166

Chapter 38 170

Chapter 39 174

Chapter 40 186

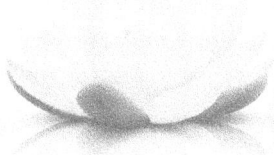

Chapter 1

Sun is hiding slowly behind the mighty mountains, turning blue colored sky to reddish orange, and another wonderful day is coming to its end; this is what Nancy felt looking out through her window and sipping a mug of hot coffee. She worked as a manager in a homeopathic company, and her job was to check the daily collection of precious herbs grown in this beautiful city of Kashmir and to report them in the head office in New Delhi. She was an American working for Edumed Homeopathic company. It was her belief that bought her here. She believed that healing was a natural process, be it of mind or body, natural products work much better than synthetic products. Here, life was much easier than her country, and she felt a strong bond with the culture, nature and simplicity here.

About six months ago, she landed on this beautiful paradise, she was unsure of her choice as she had left her promising banking career to be close to nature, and Edumed provided her the same. Sameer, a cab driver of the company received Nancy; he was about 30 years old, well built with sharp piercing eyes complemented by a roman nose. He greeted Nancy and took her luggage to the cab. She never thought that he would be his one of the closest friends. She sat quietly with thousands of questions wandering in her mind, but as she looked outside, she was mesmerized by the simplicity of the city. Within no time, she reached her guest house, which was surrounded by beautiful trees, majestic mountains, chirping birds and the freshness of air. The room shone brightly with wooden walls, bed with intricate wooden work, curtains of famous Kashmiri embroidery with blue and red flowers, a wooden table with daffodils and roses above it. Each thing complimented the other, giving a rich royal yet very simple and elegant look. This was the moment when she realized that it's the best decision she had ever made because life is very simple, but we humans make it complicated by running after money, seeking revenge, having jealousy. The reality is other way round; our world is full of beauty, love, compassion, happiness, joy.

She was about to have a nap when she heard a familiar voice coming from outside her guesthouse.

She decided to check it out. It was Daniel; what on the earth is he doing here? Is he following me? Is he on one of his honeymoons? Why do I care? All these questions were haunting her. Daniel called her name only and requested her to open the door and let him in as he had to tell her something very important. She was reluctant to trust him again after whatever he has done. How can I trust him or let in? Sameer came in and asked her, if she was having any problem? She told him to make Daniel go. Once he was gone, Sameer came to her and asked who that guy was and why he was troubling her. Taking a deep breath, she told him that he was her husband who left her all alone without any warning. Sameer was not convinced by Nancy's answer, so he asked again. Your Husband? He left you? I mean, how could he leave so promptly? This was the reason why Nancy flew from America to start a new life, and here, he came again to haunt her. She told Sameer that she didn't want to talk about it. Sameer put his hand in his pocket and gave her a beautiful stone. She was surprised after seeing the stone. She spoke with an excitement like a six-year-old kid. *Oh, my God! It's an amethyst.* I am in love with the beauty of crystals and I do have a good collection of them, but this amethyst is pure beauty. I don't know much about these stones, but I like collecting them. Although Sameer was his driver, he was her only friend here. He used to make Nancy laugh with his stupid jokes.

As he was the one with whom she used to spend a lot of time. He was a very good cook. She thanked Sameer, and he went away. Whole night she was not able to sleep and was continuously thinking about Daniel.

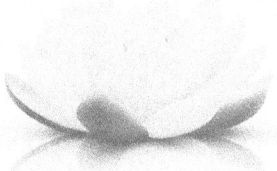

Chapter 2

She met Daniel in High school and both of them were madly in love with each other. She still remembered the smell of musk that came from Daniel. He was the son of the Mayor of Denver city; his mother had died when he was just six months old. He got all the love from Nancy, to him Nancy was all he had. Although he had a lot of money and could buy anything, still he was happy only when he was around Nancy. Theirs was a magical relationship. They could understand each other's feelings just by looking into their eyes. They stood there for each other through thick and thin. It was prom night when Daniel proposed to Nancy with balloons in one hand and a beautiful ring in the other; she immediately said yes. That was a dreamy night; she felt herself like a real-life princess. Her lavender gown complemented her blonde hair. When Daniel put a ring on her finger, her white cheeks turned red;

she couldn't believe it was all happening. It felt so wonderful. I promise you, Nancy, I will love you till my last breath. They both held hands and promised to be there for each other.

After completing high school Daniel's dad wanted him to join the prestigious college in California, but he didn't want to go, leaving Nancy. Hey Daniel, why are you so upset? We have finally finished high school; now, we can go to university together. Nancy, my dad wants me to go to, California for further studies, but I am not going anywhere. Although she didn't like his father's suggestion, she convinced Daniel for considering it as well. Daniel, maybe your father is right, give it a chance. It will be a great opportunity for you; go for it and make me proud. I don't want to leave you here and go. I just want to be with you. Daniel, I am always with you, no matter what happens. She somehow persuaded him to go. Daniel, we both have been together for many years and we do trust each other. I know this long-distance relationship will be hard for both of us, but believe me, we can do it. They both sat holding hands on a bench in Liberty Park watching birds.

Now, the time for Daniel's departure came. She went to see him off to the airport. As she saw a big blue horse with demonic red eyes staring at her, she felt as if the horse was laughing at her... He is not coming back... You are a fool, little girl, who let him go... He is not going to come back. The laughter grew louder and louder. She placed both her hands on her ears and closed her eyes tightly. Nancy... Are you OK? Asked Daniel.She didn't utter a word and hugged him. Daniel hugged her back and promised her to come back soon. You know Nancy, I always get fascinated by this blue mustang statue . Its so magnificent yet mysterious. She bid him goodbye and saw him disappearing slowly behind the doors. Something inside her broke, and she could hear screams coming from inside, but she had to put on a brave face.

She went on to study accounts at a regional college. Both of them used to talk a lot on the phone, but after one year Daniel suddenly started to avoid her. He was always ready to fight and always told her that Nancy was being too complaining, and it was her decision to send him here. Phone calls, which used to be after every hour suddenly changed to after a few days and then months; after some time there was total closure. He stopped picking up Nancy's phone calls. She even tried to contact his father, but he was too busy to meet her. Somehow, after struggling for few months, Nancy was able to move on. She never realized that she could move on so easily. After few years, she was appointed to the city bank. She bought herself a new home and a new car. Finally, after years of struggling, she stood here independently on her own. One night, she felt a sudden rush of cold breeze on her face and without wasting any second, she said, Oh, my God! Is Daniel alright? She could sense goosebumps on her arms and a nauseating feeling. She felt sick and was not able to sleep. With all her courage, she dialed his number which she still remembered. Phone rang; a similar voice received it. Her heart started to beat faster upon hearing his voice. Both were silent for two minutes and then started crying. Tears started rolling down Daniel's eyes reaching his cheeks and finally falling on the picture of Nancy that he was already holding. He told her to help him out, as she was the only one he could trust. They planned to meet in their favorite restaurant the Moonland Café. Nancy reached there before time, as she was excited and worried at the same time. Thousands of thoughts were wandering in her mind, and suddenly, Daniel entered through that door. He was not the same Daniel whom she loved. He was changed from fit to fat, indicating his unhealthy lifestyle; still, those eyes and smile were the same. She was able to look into his soul through his eyes. He appeared a weak and fragile Daniel, hiding beneath those extra layers of fat. He hugged her and continuously looked into her eyes as if he was asking for forgiveness. He told her not to hide her hands as he had already seen that she was still wearing that ring which he had given to her in High school. A waiter came to their seat for their order and both simultaneously said margarita pizza with extra cheese and then looked into each other's eyes. Nancy's eyes were asking so many questions to Daniel. Finally, Daniel told her that he was forced into drugs, and now, he wants to leave it as drugs have snatched everything from him. He had become a womanizer now; a druggie, with whom nobody wanted to talk. He was totally devastated and begged Nancy to help him. Something was there in Daniel that Nancy couldn't resist. She wiped his tears and promised to help him in every possible way. After a few days, Nancy got him admitted to a rehabilitation center and provided emotional and psychological support. Daniel started working in a software company, and they got married within a few months. Nancy was expecting her first child with Daniel and was so excited to share this news with him. She came home and waited for Daniel, but Daniel didn't come, only a note was there; as she opened the note on a big piece of paper, the only thing which was written was SORRY. Nancy was shocked, and she waited every day for him to return, but he didn't. This time, she was not able to move on. Then she decided to do it for her child. Throughout her pregnancy, she waited for him. On her routine visits to Gynecologists, the mere presence of other couples nauseated her. There was no one to hold her hands, no one to talk and no one to share her feelings with. On her seventh-month scan, Dr. told Nancy that her baby was not growing properly, and there was growth restriction, which might lead to certain problems. Nancy was distraught that night. She wanted that baby desperately. On 22 June, she felt labor pain and her water broke. She was immediately taken to hospital where she delivered a beautiful daughter. Her sparking angelic eyes took away her breath; her nose was definitely of Daniel. The moment she took her daughter in her arms, she felt flood of unconditional love. It was during this moment that she forgot about Daniel and her heart was filled with love for her daughter, but her happiness was short-lived. Doctors told her that her daughter needs immediate care, and she should be admitted to the NICU. Nancy was unable to understand what was going on. They took her daughter away and told her to relax. After two hours, doctors told her that they couldn't save her daughter. In just few minutes, life turned upside down for her. She was not crying just numb, holding the dead body of her daughter, touching her face, kissing her. How could she leave me just like this? She was with me just two hours ago, and now, she's gone. Doctor, please check, she might be asleep; please wake her up, she said helplessly. She came home empty-handed and locked herself in her house. After two months, she tried to gather her strength back and joined the bank again. She could feel the questions and pity feeling of her colleagues towards her; she was not comfortable with that. It was not the same Nancy; she didn't talk much nor did she go to parties.

Once, the most talkative girl was now an expressionless person, just sitting in front of the system and working. One of her colleagues Emma told her about the newly opened meditation and healing center in the city and suggested her to visit it once. She turned herself in the Art of Meditation classes and learned about meditation and the use of crystals for healing. Suddenly, the house which was full of accountancy books got replaced by crystals of all sorts: clear quartz, rose quartz, amethyst, tiger eye and many more, and also the books of all sorts of psychic healing. She felt better now and slowly she was returning to her normal life, but for her, some things were changed forever, money had the least importance in her life now. She wanted to live with empathy, so she left her job and joined Edumed Homeopathic company, an Indian company which was not that famous, but this company provided her with change which was the utmost requirement of the time.

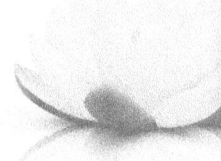

Chapter 3

Birds started chirping, darkness was being replaced by soft light; Nancy just realized that she had not slept the whole night and was thinking about Daniel. She got up and looked out through the window at how dawn was taking over darkness. She sat on her mat and closed her eyes with her hands folded. With every inhale she felt a rush of positive energy and with exhale she imagined all the negativity leaving her body. Usually, she was able to meditate for half an hour, but today she could just sit for ten minutes, still, thinking about Daniel. She heard the honking of the car; this was the usual way of Sameer when he came to pick her up for the site. She took important files with her and locked the door and sat in the cab. So, Mam today we are going to a new site for collecting orange gold said Sameer in a funny tone. Nancy looked at him with a confused look, orange gold? When did Edumed start collecting gold? Sameer smirked and said Mam I mean saffron. We are going to collect saffron today. It's one of the specialties of Kashmir. Nancy smiled and looked out through the window; majestic river Jhelum was flowing with utmost silence; no sound could be heard. She thought how similar she and Jhelum were, so silent on the outside, but carrying turbulence of emotions within. It was her meditation that allowed her to feel and resonate with nature. The car stopped with a powerful brake bringing Nancy to the real world. Sorry Mam, a calf came between the road, and I had to stop, said Sameer apologetically. He parked the car outside the field. She stepped out of the car and looked at the saffron fields which were covered by violet flowers. The flowers were so delicate with violet petals and orange anthers. Sameer showed her the fields and introduced her to the owner of the field, who was ready to sell his flowers to the company. Nice to meet you, sir. You have a beautiful field. Look at these flowers; they are so beautiful, Nancy said with a smile on her face. The owner didn't understand a word, but he just placed his hand on her head and left reciprocating the same smile. Sameer started with her similar way. So, now you have the blessing of an old man, not any ordinary man, but the owner of this field, what on earth do you need now? Your purpose on earth is now fulfilled. Nancy looked at him, and they both laughed until tears started rolling down her eyes. How can you find humor in any situation? You must be a very happy and lucky man, Nancy said looking into his eyes. He replied instantly... Oh! Yes, Mam, I am a very lucky man and I am content with whatever I have. It was for the first time, she felt as if whatever Sameer was saying was true other way around. Third eye chakra, isn't it? Nancy said looking into the vast field. Sameer was startled. What's that? And yes, purple is the color for the third eye chakra. That's why my intuition is telling me that you are hiding something. Sameer was an expert in masking. He handed over the file to her, which had to be filled regarding the collection of saffron and both became busy with their work. While returning from the site, Nancy was still busy looking into her file. Sameer gathered his strength to ask her, Mam what do you think why your husband wants to meet you? Nancy's face turned red, goosebumps on her arms and tears started filling her eyes. She was unable to answer his question. A tear rolled from her eyes over the file followed by a rain of tears. She closed the file and sat quietly looking out through the window. Sameer felt very bad about what he just did to her. Mam, I didn't mean to hurt you. Sameer, you are just a driver here, don't try to get personal with me. Sameer was taken aback by Nancy's words. He didn't utter a word and kept calm. Upon reaching the guest house, Nancy just stepped out of the car without saying goodbye to him.

Nancy saw a letter outside her door. She took it and went inside her room. The letter was from Daniel. She opened it… Please meet me. I will wait for you in the alley behind your guest house at 10 pm. Nancy crushed the paper and threw it on the floor. When I needed him, he ran away. I supported him through difficult times, and he left me and our daughter. Our angel died, but his father was too busy somewhere else that he didn't even come to her funeral. I don't want to see his face. She said with anger in her eyes. Love never dies, but only takes a back seat. She opened the letter again and decided to go. Her heart started beating faster as the clock struck 10. She stood up from her chair and started walking outside. It was so dark out there, with owls cooing and distinct howling adding up to the uncomfortable eerie. She stood there in the alley waiting for Daniel. She saw two men approaching her. She hid on the side of a giant chinar tree. As the men came closer, she saw one man giving some packets to the other and told him something in a regional language. Although Nancy was learning Kashmiri language but she was not able to decipher , she felt something fishy. As the men left, she felt a presence behind her, she was too scared to turn but slowly turned back, and as she turned it was Daniel. What do you think you are doing, and how could you expect me to talk to you after all the pain you gave me, said Nancy with anger. You left me when I was expecting a child, and even that angel left me. Daniel felt as if a heavy load was put on his heart. He was about to fall. We had a child? What happened to our baby? What is the point of asking such questions now? I lost my everything, said Nancy crying. Daniel held his head and sat down on the ground. I am guilty; I don't know how to repent. I can't imagine what you have gone through, please forgive me.He wiped his tears and pulled himself together and said, look, Nancy I don't have much time, but please leave this place as soon as possible, It's not that what you are seeing. Go back to Denver, said Daniel. Nancy was not able to react and was standing like a lifeless creature. Daniel kissed her hand and said I love you, Nancy. I really do; please try to understand. Suddenly, he left her hand and told her to go back to her guest room this instant and not to open it for anybody. She came back, sat on the bed and was still in shock about what just happened.

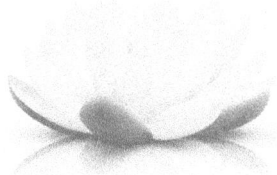

Chapter 4

The warmth of the sun was kissing her face; she opened her eyes and welcomed this day with a big smile on her face. Her mind kept repeating the words of Daniel. I love you, Nancy. I really do. She looked at the hand where he planted a kiss. An ultimate sense of happiness filled her mind and body. She did her meditation and got ready for the site with a big smile on her face. She saw Sameer from her window, and today, for a change, no honking was needed, she went straight to Sameer and hugged him. She told him that she was sorry for yesterday's behavior. Sameer froze there, as being hugged by a girl was not common in his culture. For the first time, Sameer who was otherwise a witty parrot turned into a sloppy turtle. He drove the car with utmost silence while Nancy was continuously talking. On reaching the field, she realized that apart from 'I love you' there was something else which

Daniel told her. Why does he want me to leave this place? What could possibly go wrong? Who were those two men, I saw exchanging packets and what did Daniel actually see which made him tell me not to open door to anybody? She went straight to Sameer and asked him. Is there anything for her to worry about here? Sameer looked confused and told her, Mam why are you behaving so different today? Why are you asking these questions? Are you Nancy or somebody else? Nancy didn't want to tell Sameer about what Daniel told her. So, she just changed the topic. Oh, Sameer, you never introduced me to your family. Do you want to meet my family? I would love to take you there, but… Sameer stopped. Nancy immediately interrupted, what do you mean by but, I want to go there, so take me there. It will be my honor, but we are not that rich. You will not be comfortable there, Sameer said with a gloomy face. On hearing this, Nancy laughed and said, do you really think money matters? It's just an illusion dear to keep us humans busy. Now, I owe you a crystal, she took out a clear quartz crystal from her bag and gave it to Sameer. I am giving you this so that you can see clearly what matters and what does not. It's a weekend, so we can go today. Perfect said Nancy. They both smiled and looked towards the horizon.

She sat in the cab and they moved towards Sameer's village. The road was surrounded by lush green fields and strong trees; yellow mustard fields somewhere were adding charm to this beautiful place. Oh, Sameer, you were so mean not bringing me here in the first place. She said mesmerized by the beauty. It was already dark when they reached his place. They went inside and were greeted by Sameer's mother and younger sister. A typical Kashmiri food was served to them. Mam, you must be tired, I must take you to your room. She stood up and both went upstairs. There was no light upstairs, so he lit a candle in her room and left. She woke up early morning, looking out through that broken window. It was the most beautiful and satisfying vision, she had ever seen. Lush green grass with beautiful red and orange flowers, clear blue sky and voices of cattle and hens gave her a sense of relaxation. Sameer knocked at the door. Oh, come in, Sameer. Thank you for allowing me to come here. Sameer smiled and told her, I bought you something. So, which crystal is it today a bloodstone or turquoise, asked Nancy smiling. No, it's not a crystal, it's a dress; I bought our Kashmiri traditional dress for you. Sameer handed over the dress to her. The dress was white with beautiful flowers within it and an overlying tunic, which they called pheren, was of green velvet with motif and pearl embroidery over the neck. It's so beautiful; I would love to wear it, said Nancy, hugging Sameer. He again blushed.

They both went for a stroll in the village. The view was far from what villages, she had seen in her country. Some houses didn't even have the basic necessities. Despite being so backwards, the people were happy and carefree and were carrying genuine smiles on their faces. Children were looking at Nancy with excitement; some girls even came forward to touch her hand. She had never received so much importance in her life. At this point, she realized that beauty comes from within and lies in the eyes of the beholder. These children are so innocent and happy. I wish I could have that same genuine smile, said Nancy looking at the children. Mam, you do have a very beautiful smile and for these children, you are not less than any Bollywood star, said Sameer looking into Nancy's eyes. The weekend was over, and they had to report to the site early in the morning. They bid adieu to Sameer's mother and sister and went straight to the site.

You will damage saffron flowers; please be careful, said Nancy to a new worker. He looked towards her and continued to pluck flowers. This man is so rude; I think I have seen him somewhere. Oh! Why can't I remember it? She continuously thought about that man while sitting quietly on a wooden log. Sameer noticed her sitting all alone quietly thinking about something. He came to her and told her, so, what's the plan now? She looked towards him, puzzled. Plan? What kind of plan? Oh, you are sitting so quietly. I thought you might be planning to kill somebody, said Sameer sarcastically. I think I have seen that man in the green shirt somewhere, but I am not able to remember, where, replied Nancy.

That man with green shirt is Ravi. He is from Bihar and works as a daily wager, said Sameer. This, Ravi, is very rude; I told him to pluck flowers carefully, he didn't even bother to reply, said Nancy feeling agitated. Sameer started to laugh as hard as possible. Mam, I think you need Clear quartz crystal more than I do; even if you will kill him, he will not say anything because he is deaf and dumb.

Nancy began to feel sorry for Ravi, but there was something about Ravi that was not letting her think about anything else. She did not receive good vibes from him. Suddenly, she remembered what Daniel had said: "This place is not safe. Go away from here." She somehow felt something, somewhere was terribly wrong. Another day came to an end, and they drove towards the guesthouse. Her mind was still preoccupied with thoughts of Ravi. He didn't look like a daily wager. His clothes were neat and clean, and he carried pair of branded shoes.

Nancy: Branded shoes?

Sameer: You want to buy branded shoes?

Nancy: Oh, no Sameer. You are telling me that he was a daily wager, but he didn't look like one. I mean, look at other workers and their clothing. He was totally different from them, also, he was wearing pair of branded shoes.

Sameer: Mam this is India and here, we can easily get a copy of expensive branded things in a very affordable rate, or somebody might have given it to him. Why are you thinking about him so much?

Oh, I got it, you have found the love of your life in Ravi. Nancy was not in the mood to laugh at Sameer's stupid jokes. She kept looking out of the window; upon reaching, she said goodbye to Sameer and went inside her guest house. When she opened the door, she felt as if somebody else was also there. She could hear the sound of stuff being thrown away here and there. She went slowly into the kitchen to fetch a knife. As she entered her bedroom, she saw a man in a black hoodie with his face covered in a mask. Nancy screamed as high as she could, that man jumped through the kitchen window, and Sameer came rushing to her.

Sameer: Are you alright? What happened?

Nancy: I don't know. I saw a man in my room and he jumped out of the window. I can't live in this guest house; it's not safe at all.

Sameer: Don't worry! Mam, we will find out who was the intruder, and you don't worry. I will arrange your stay in another guest house.

Nancy was so terrified; her whole body was shivering, I am not safe here, I am not safe here, she was continuously repeating it. Sameer reassured her that he will guard her today and tomorrow. She will be moved to the next Guest house. Nancy agreed.

Do you want a glass of water? Asked Sameer. No. No, I am fine. Daniel was right, I am not safe here. I came here to live my life peacefully, but look, nobody wants me to be happy, said Nancy.

Why are you overthinking, He must be a thief, who might have thought that let's rob a foreigner, said Sameer trying to lift her mood. Nancy didn't seem to be in the mood to laugh. She kept staring at a wall. "Who might that person be? What was Daniel warning me about? Is there something really bad going to happen? Is Sameer not realizing the actual depth of situation or is he involved too? I don't know and I can't trust anyone. I need to find it myself," thought Nancy.

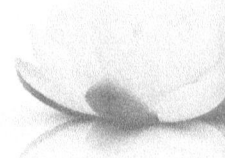

Chapter 5

The clock struck 10; something inside Nancy told her to go out to the same place where she met Daniel. She sneaked out of the main door silently and stood there by that giant tree. Those two men, whom she saw the other day returned and exchanged packets. As she looked closely, she observed that it was Ravi with some other man. Ravi was talking to that man. The only thing she heard was "charas." After sometime, those two men went away, and she stood there silently thinking what the meaning of charas is. She suddenly realized that Ravi was actually talking. He was not deaf and dumb; instead he was fooling everybody. She felt as if somebody was standing behind her, as she turned it was Sameer.

Sameer (whispering): So, James Bond, what are you doing here? Is your mission accomplished? Can we go to the guest house, now?

Nancy: You won't believe what I just saw; Ravi could actually talk.

Sameer: Mam you are too tired and terrified. Let's go back and talk there. They went to the guest house. Nancy was furious with Sameer for not understanding her. She told him that she was not lying, it was Ravi, but Sameer was not ready to listen. So, she stood up, went to her bedroom and slept. Next morning, when they were heading to site, there was complete silence in the cab. Neither Sameer nor Nancy talked about anything. Upon reaching the site, Nancy's eyes were searching for Ravi, and there he was looking at a field with a suspicious look. Nancy went to him and spoke. Are you not going to pluck flowers today? He looked towards her and showed her gestures that he can't listen to or speak. To which Nancy smirked and said LIAR. Ravi looked into Nancy's eyes and gave her a cunning smile. Then he went on to pluck flowers. Sameer came to Nancy and told her to leave Ravi alone. Mam, this is not fair, you can't keep irritating a physically impaired person. Nancy smiled and left. She knew back in her mind that there was much going on below the surface. She kept observing Ravi. He had an average build and average height. His skin color was a bit darker than other workers. His shirt was tucked in his jeans, with nice pair of shoes and he must be in his late thirties or early forties. Suddenly, he stood up and went to the other side of the field and came back after fifteen minutes. He was not just any ordinary worker, but a suspicious man who was camouflaging his reality. On her way home, Sameer told Nancy that he considered Ravi as his elder brother and didn't like anybody troubling him. Nancy was disappointed on hearing those words. She closed her eyes pretending to having a nap. Her mind was flooded with thoughts of all sorts and was, again and again, replaying the words of Daniel "Go away from here, you are not safe here". They were struck in a traffic jam, she didn't want to talk to Sameer, so she looked outside the window; she saw an elderly man in his sixties carving stones, there were beautifully carved mortar pestles in his shop, and with those same stones, he was making tombstones. We are all made up of that same stone, but depend upon how they tame themselves. It's all in our hands to decide which way to go. Everybody seems to stand on the fork of the road at some point in their life, our choices make us the person we are now. She decided not to judge Sameer as it was his choice how he chose to shape his life.

Sameer: Mam, please pack your luggage as we are leaving for another guest house.

Nancy: No, it's alright; I don't want to leave now.

Sameer: Are you sure, Mam? Should I stay with you?

Nancy: No, thanks. I am fine. Do come to get me in the morning, goodbye.

Sameer stood there confused as to why she opted to stay in this guest house while yesterday she wanted to leave this place as soon as possible.

"It's really hard to unlock a girl's mind, no matter from which country she belonged," exclaimed Sameer.

The night started to unfold itself; everything bright was just being overpowered by the darkness, distant sounds of animals were arriving. She sat on the chair, looking out of the window, holding a cup of hot coffee. She saw a man, covering his face with a hood, standing outside the gate of the guest house. She was alarmed to see him. She stood up slowly, closed the lights and hid behind the curtains. Her breath was getting heavier and heavier with every passing second. She looked again from behind the curtains towards the gate; Now, no one was there. He was gone. She drank a glass of water, still shaking with fear. She sat on the chair near the window with lights closed. After ten minutes, she saw a man again, who was hiding in the bushes, outside her guest house.

She gathered her strength and threw the glass, she was holding, on to the man hiding under the bushes. It hit the man, and he ran away. Nancy didn't dare to get up and go to the bed; she was sitting on the chair holding knife.

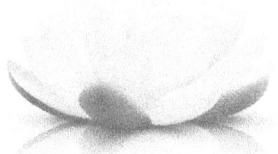

Chapter 6

The Driver quarters were a few meters from the guest house. They were two-room sets with modest furniture, single bed with warm bedsheet, steel wardrobe at the corner of the room, old curtains covering the windows, including a small kitchen with basic utensils and a gas stove. Sameer was restlessly looking here and there in his drawer, taking things out of it and throwing them on the floor. He held his head in despair. He took a deep breath and started sorting his belongings. He picked out a silver ring with a big rounded pearl, kissed the ring and started crying like a small kid. "No, No, not again… Please stay away, Nancy". He wiped his tears and lighted a cigarette and stared at the empty wall. Suddenly, he felt a sharp pain in his fingers. It was the butt of the cigarette; he threw it on the floor. "I need to stop this as soon as possible; Nancy is such an adamant lady, she is not ready to listen to anything. I have to make her believe that everything is normal here."

Sameer tried to sleep, but the images of that ring haunted him, and he was not able to sleep. He turned to another side, but the devil of insomnia did not let him sleep. He was lying motionless, staring at the ceiling. He heard a knock at the door; he tried to get off the bed but was not able to. Knock grew stronger and stronger, but Sameer could not get up. After some time, there was complete silence, He could feel sweat flowing down his face. A beautiful lady in a green velvet pheran was standing beside him and smiling. How did you come in? Am I not welcome in your home, now? Asked the lady. Help me; I am not able to move. Why should I help you? Did you help my fiancé? Did you help your brother…? No you just ran away… You are a coward. Sameer put his hands across his ears to stop hearing her voice... Please stop it... I beg you; I did everything I could; I am not a coward; please stop. No Sameer, you ruined my life and now, you want to sleep peacefully. Sameer begged the lady to stop and was crying badly. Sameer? Sameer? Wake up! Wake up! Another driver who was living in the nearby quarter tried to wake him up. Sameer woke up, realizing it was just a dream. Please drink this water. Sameer drank it. I think you saw a nightmare Yes... I heard your screams and saw you were screaming in sleep, so I thought to wake you up. Thanks a lot, friend. Sameer stood up and went outside. Where are you going? It's still dark. Sameer left without answering him.

Chapter 7

Glowing light started filling the room; Nancy could feel the warmth of the sun on her face. Her neck ached due to improper sleeping position. Within no time, Sameer came with the cab. Today, Nancy decided not to tell Sameer about it. Sameer was looking tired as if he had also not slept the whole night. He asked her Mam, were you alright last night? Nancy replied, trying to be as casual as possible, oh, yeah! Everything was fine. Nancy caught Sameer when he was looking towards her. Through the front mirror. Nancy: What happened? Why are you looking at me?

Sameer: Nothing, I am not looking at you.

After reaching the site, both were walking towards the field. When Sameer was about to place his foot on cow dung, Nancy held his arm to stop him.

Sameer screamed in pain as his arm was injured.

Nancy: What happened to your arm Sameer?

Sameer: Oh, I fell from the stairs.

Nancy: Show me. Are you sure? It looks like a wound caused by a sharp object, not by a blunt object.

Sameer: May be there was something sharp on the stairs. You tell me; are you going to change your guest house?

Nancy: No, I am looking for something, and I think I am very close to find it, so I am not going anywhere.

Sameer: Nothing is wrong here, so don't waste your energy digging problems, which don't even exist.

Nancy walked away without listening to Sameer and continued to enter something on her file. Today, Ravi didn't come to work, and it was their last day of collecting saffron. She sat on her favorite log sitting quietly and tried to relate things which were happening. Where is Daniel? Is he alright? What is going on and what are these people hiding? Why is Sameer protecting them? Does he know something? Nancy closed her eyes, and imagined herself as an angel with wings flying in the beautiful sky, above the green trees, colorful flowers and majestic rivers. Suddenly, she felt as if somebody tore her wings and she was falling towards the surface. She opened her eyes when somebody caught her. Sameer was standing there, trying to wake her up and was holding her hand.

Sameer: Are you alright? I saw you were gnawing Nancy told him that she was watching a dream, maybe; that's why, she was gnawing.

Nancy: Do you know where my husband is staying?

Sameer: How would I know? And, by the way, he has caused immense pain to you. Why are you even bothered about him? There is no need to find him.

Nancy: How dare you speak like this about my husband. Who are you to tell me what to do and what not to?

Sameer lowered his gaze and apologized for his behavior.

Nancy entered her guest room, kept the files on the table and sat totally disheartened. What is going on; why I am struck here? I think I should go back to Denver. Where is Daniel? I can't leave him here all alone, Daniel knows whatever is going on. He is in trouble, I can't leave him here and go. Nancy decided to go out of the guest house for a stroll. The cold breeze was kissing her face softly, her hair was moving with the music of the breeze. Houseboats, mesmerizing Dal Lake, and innocent people were walking and smiling. Everything was so breathtaking that for a while, she forgot what was going on in her life. Suddenly, she felt as if somebody was following her; she didn't dare to turn back but continued to walk forward. She saw a park on the left side of the road; she went inside and sat on a bench where a lady was sitting. Nancy was continuously looking here and there to check whether that man has left or not. In this beautiful weather, she was sweating a lot. Are you alright, asked the other woman? Yeah, totally, replied Nancy. Hi, I am Sara and these are my kids, she said pointing towards two boys playing in the park. My name is Nancy. Sara leaned towards Nancy and said, "Isn't this place beautiful?" Nancy tried to fake a smile. You want water? No, thanks, said Nancy, clearing her throat. Are you a tourist, said Sara? No, I am not a tourist; I work here for a company. Nancy kept on looking here and there. Where are you from Nancy? I am from the U.S. You came from the U.S to work here? I mean everybody goes from our country to the U.S.; I have never been to the U.S, but would love to go there. Sure, but your paradise is very beautiful. Indeed, said Sara. You might be thinking why I am asking so many questions. Nancy checked her watch, "It's getting late? I should reach the guest house before dark." Sara decided to walk with Nancy to her guest house. Nancy didn't want to go alone, so she agreed. "What do you do Sara?" I am a housewife, but I have done BAMS, said Sara with a sigh. You are a ayurvedic doctor? So, why don't you practice? "After marriage, priorities change, my whole world revolves around these kids only, but sometimes, I do feel disheartened for not continuing my career," said Sara with a gloomy face. Upon reaching the guest house, both the women decided to meet at 5 the next day, Sara and the kids waved to Nancy and left.

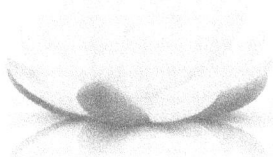

Chapter 8

Next morning, she woke up early. While find out that Sameer had already arrived and was waiting in the cab, she looked at the clock... It's only 5 am... what is he doing here? I should get ready. She did her morning meditation and went to Sameer. He opened the car's door for her. There was complete silence in the cab. Where are we going today, asked Nancy, trying to break the silence? We are going to a different site today, and it's a bit far from here, so we had to leave earlier, replied Sameer. They reached the site one hour before time. It was a beautiful garden full of fig trees, decorated by bulb-shaped, pinkish-purple figs. Nancy smiled, looking at the beauty of this place, "Look, Sameer it's so peaceful and calm here." Sameer tried to look into Nancy's eyes, "Yeah, this place is peaceful, but are you calm and peaceful? Nancy tried to avoid this conversation by turning her face away from Sameer. He pulled her closer to him "Nancy, I don't want anything bad happens to you, please, don't put your nose in everything." Nancy was not able to move or reply. Sameer realized that he held her too tight and too close. He immediately let her loose and apologized for what he just did. I am sorry, I don't know what got over me, please forgive me. Nancy slapped him as hard as possible. I knew you know a lot more than you show, and it was you who came to the guesthouse that night, the wound you got clearly proved it. You are a disgusting piece of SH... t. I never considered you as a mere driver... I considered you as a friend, but you were a pal hole in disguise. I don't want to see your filthy face anymore. Go away. Soon, all the workers gathered there, Nancy called the head office and reported the need for a change of driver. She was allotted a new driver, and Sameer was fired out of his job.

In the evening, she met Sara in the same park where they had met last day. You look worried, said Sara. I came here to run away from my problems, but I think they also boarded the plane from U.S to here. Sara held her hand and reassured her that everything would be fine. Nancy, there were many times when being a female, I had to pay the cost, but the only thing, which kept me going was my faith in myself and diversion. Nancy looked confused... Diversion?? Yes, I mean... people usually tell you that not to run from your fears and face them, but in reality, the more you ignore the things which haunt you, the better it gets. All the fears are not meant to be dealt with spades and arrows; some are to be dealt with brain. Train your brain to filter these junks, and you will see the world with beauty. See, you had also come to Kashmir to divert yourself from the pain you had in the U.S. This time also, you have to do the same, divert your mind from things, which are not good for your mental peace and focus on things, which make you feel better. It's not easy to always run Sara, I have always done this, but today, something different happened, the person I considered my friend was actually a foe. If you don't mind, can you tell me what happened? Nancy smiled softly and told her what happened today. Nancy, do you think what his hidden motive was? May be, he was actually protecting you. Protecting me, from what? That I don't know, but whatever be the reason, he should not have held you. Nobody has the right to cross boundaries. Sometimes, during winter days before snowfall, everything looks dark, but eventually after the snowfall everything gets shiny and bright; so bright that we need to put our glares on. So, just wait and see one day, the truth will unfold, and you, too, will see clearly, until then "DIVERSION." Nancy was still not satisfied with her reassurance, "He was the only friend I had here, but I can't let him abuse me. I miss him." Sara tried to comfort her "Why don't you come to my place for dinner. You are alone and must be missing your family." Nancy was reluctant at first but finally agreed. They both went to Sara's place. The mansion was beautiful and big. She lived with her in-laws in a beautiful mansion on the banks of Dal. Sara led Nancy to the guestroom and introduced Nancy to her husband Amir, who was a cop, and to her in laws. They were watching the news, and suddenly, news flashed about the secret drug menace in the valley. Cops have arrested a foreign man named Gabriel from Denver. Sara's father-in-law spoke in distraught, "What is happening to our paradise, this drug disease will slowly engulf all the Kashmir. No one will be spared if any strict actions are not taken on time." You are from which city, Nancy? Nancy reluctantly said, Denver. Sara called everyone to the dinner table. After dinning, Sara's husband went to drop Nancy at her guest house. He was a tall, well-built, muscular man. Upon reaching her guest house, Amir told Nancy that it was for the first time in years he had seen Sara so happy. Sara seems to be a happy lady. Yeah, she seems to be one but is not. I sometimes feel I am not able to give her the happiness, which she deserves. Do keep coming. As Nancy was about to step out of the car, he asked her to stop. There is somebody hiding behind the bushes, just sit in the car, I will see. Amir slowly got out of the car and went behind the bushes. That man tried to run away but was caught by him. Who are you and what are you doing here, he asked him? The man was constantly trying to hide his face. When Nancy got a glimpse of him, She was not able to believe her eyes. "Sameer? What on earth are you doing here?" You know him, asked Amir. Nancy told him that Sameer was her cab driver. I am going to put him in jail and you go inside the guesthouse, said Amir authoritatively.

Chapter 9

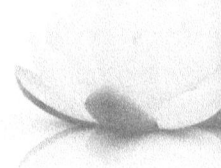

Life is like a knife, the more you grind it, the sharper it gets, Nancy had to come so far from her country in search of peace and tranquility, but it seemed as if life was testing her with more turbulence. Today was hectic day for Nancy and unpredictable too. Nancy was continuously thinking about Sameer. "Innocent faces could do such harm, he was the one behind everything, may be, that's why he was protecting Ravi." I have to search Daniel; where is he? How did he know something was wrong here?" The next day, after returning from her site, she went to meet Sara and Amir. We have kept Sameer in our custody, but he will be out in a few days, as we have no proof against him. He gave a statement that he was strolling in that area, and his ring fell; he was looking for it behind the bushes, and you know, he was in jail about 5 years ago for drug peddling and he was even suspected of killing his brother. Suspect of murder, exclaimed Nancy?? I could have never believed it if someone else had told me. I wonder how the companies could hire such persons, said Amir, distraught. What about that foreign male named Gabriel who was arrested yesterday, asked Nancy with hesitation. Oh, that man from your city? "He is yet to open his mouth, but his brother hired a lawyer to look into his case," replied Amir while eating an apple. Brother? His brother is also here? Nancy asked. "Yeah! I forgot his name, what was it? I am very bad with names; I think it was Michael… Oh, no wait. It was Daniel... Yes, his name was Daniel, and you know, he was the son of the ex-mayor of Denver city. See, what a disgrace!" Nancy felt as if she is been falling from the sky, her husband had a brother, and she had no clue about him, but at least, she was content that now she could reach Daniel. Nancy was spellbound, unable to move or react. Are you alright, Nancy, Sara asked? He is my husband, said Nancy. Amir stopped munching the apple, and there was complete silence. Sara interrupted to avoid awkwardness; I am bored by both of you. Can we please eat something or go outside, remarked Sara? All of them went outside for a stroll and dropped Nancy back at guest house. Sara and Nancy got out of the car. Life is a very tough examiner, sometimes this examiner asks out-of-syllabus questions for which we are never prepared, so the best thing to do is attempt the questions you know and leave those which you don't know. Sara, it's not that easy, getting to know that your husband had a brother whom you were not aware of. It shows how less I know about him. You will get all your answers and you deserve to know them. Believe me, you will get to know everything. Sara hugged her and sat back in her car. Nancy grabbed the key from her purse and opened the door. She kept her bag on the table and sat on the recliner with folded hands; she was unable to move. Is this really happening or is it just a weird dream? Do I really know Daniel, thought Nancy? She gathered herself and went to bed.

The next morning, Nancy woke up, but she felt as if her mind was still sleeping, fully occupied by thoughts of all sorts, I need to meet Daniel anyhow. I think Amir would be of any help, swinging herself off the bed. Nancy got ready and went with her driver to the site, it was on the outskirts of, a very hilly area with limited greenery, she looked puzzled as to what they had to extract today. The driver went to park the taxi. She started analyzing the limited flora which was present there. She saw that a man was standing all alone and looking at her. Is he Ravi? There was nobody except herself and Ravi. She started to move towards the parking area. Ravi shouted… Madam, there is no use of running from me. I know you wanted to know about me, so here, I offer you a chance. Nancy was trembling with fear. Now, you are terrified? You wanted to know whether I could speak or not. See, I could speak so many languages, which one you wanted to hear? You don't know how much loss you have done to my business, said Ravi in a sarcastic tone. I am not afraid of you. I will report a complaint against you, said Nancy, hiding her fear. Nancy. You can only report if I will let you go. "Tell me, what do you know about us and our business?" I don't know anything. If you don't know anything, what the hell do you do outside the guest house at night? I have seen you myself. Nancy asked distraught, why are you targeting me? I came here to give my life a new start, why are you involving me in this shit? You, yourself, got into it. Who told you to become Sherlock Holmes? See, Nancy, if you want to go, you will have to do one little favor for me. No I am not going to work for you. OK! Then, get ready to die and I will make sure that you will soon meet Daniel there. Nancy was astonished to hear Daniel's name. How do you know about Daniel? Will you work for me or not? Nancy was left with no option. She had to agree to save herself and Daniel. Ok! What will I have to do? Very good! I will let you know. Don't tell anybody what we talked about; otherwise you better know what I will do? Slowly, other workers started coming, and Ravi left the site.

After returning from the site, Nancy went straight to Sara. You look stressed; what happened, enquired Sara? "I don't understand whatever is happening, but it's not good." Sara looked at Nancy and held her hands, what's the problem, Nancy? Nancy didn't want to tell Sara all this, as her husband was a police officer. Nothing Sara, I am too tired of the turbulences going on in my life. There is a good news for you; I have arranged our meeting with Gabriel and from him, we could get the address of Daniel." Nancy looked up with watery eyes, I was about to ask you the same. You don't know how much you have helped me. She stood up, and both hugged. I am feeling hungry; can we please eat something, said Sara? Sure, darling. Both of them were holding cups of Khawa, a special tea of Kashmir and Kashmiri bread. Umm! Its flavors of cardamom, cinnamon and saffron are filling my senses, and rejuvenating me. No, darling, it's the magic of my hands, said Sara, winking her eyes. C'mon! Finish your tea quickly; we have to meet Gabriel today. "Yeah sure," said Nancy, trying to drink as quickly as possible.

They entered the jail premises; Amir was waiting for them. You both are almost ten minutes late. C'mon, let's not waste time. Amir led Nancy to the cell where Gabriel was. He was a tall, lean man, with lots of tattoos and a piercing nose ring in the septum of his nose, a tattoo of a cross over his chest, skull on his right arm and written Rebecca on the left arm.

Nancy, don't be judgmental, no, no don't do this. Nancy kept on thinking. Oh, my-my look, who is here, said Gabriel with a devilish smile on his face. "Do you know me?" Of course, you are my brother's wife. Daniel never mentioned about you. I am not surprised he was always been ashamed of me, that swine got all the benefits and all the love; and you know what, he is a thief "No, you are lying." He stole my mom's love from me. I wish I could have killed him. Stop this nonsense and tell me, what are you doing here, and where is Daniel? Your Daniel has ruined my life; I thought he might be living with you, so I came to your place, but you returned and I had to run. It was you? If you could have come through the door, we could talk like how normal decent adults do. Keep your decency to yourself and tell Daniel whatever he is trying to get me out will not be helpful for him, as I will kill him as soon as I will get out of here. He started laughing like a psychotic person. Amir came and told Nancy to come with him. As she was moving through the corridor of prison, she could still hear Gabriel's frantic laughter.

She was sitting in Amir's office; suddenly, her heart started beating faster than ever when she heard a familiar voice; and tears started rolling in her eyes. She stood up and went after the voice. Daniel was sitting with another cop showing him some papers. "Daniel." "Nancy what are you doing here." "I have so much to ask you, I don't know what is happening.

Please help me, Daniel." Sweats were flowing on Daniel's forehead. "Why did you come here? I will tell you about everything, but for now, please go." "I am not going anywhere; I want answers right now, why didn't you ever tell me about Gabriel? What are you doing here, and what is going on?" It's not that simple Nancy. Trust me, I will tell you everything but please go from here. I will contact you myself; right now I must meet Gabriel, and you should leave. Nancy left with Sara and Amir. On the way, she felt as if someone was following them. As she turned back, she saw Ravi on a bike, following them. Amir, can you please drive fast, I think this man is following us. Who? No, this guy is not following us, but he is our new guard, his name is Rehman. It's his duty to follow us. Nancy felt as if she was sinking into the car seat. For how long do you know this guy? I don't know him, we just met this morning, when my earlier guard was transferred to some other place and I got this one. Nancy was shaking with fear. Amir, can you please arrange a ticket to Denver? I am missing my place; I think I should go there for some time. Sure, I will arrange it and let you know.

Chapter 10

Amir and Sara dropped Nancy off and went back home. Kids were playing carrom board with their grandparents. Come on, Papa and Mummy, play with us. Sara held the striker in her hand and was about to strike when her mother-in-law said, are we going to have dinner today or do you want us to eat carrom board? No, mummy, I am going into the kitchen. Then, go fast. Sara left the striker down and went straight to the kitchen. As she was cooking, she heard her family members laughing and giggling while playing the game. She closed the kitchen door and sat down for some time, realizing what her value is. She remembered how pampered child she was; how ambitious she was, and what she had become now. She gathered herself and cooked mutton and rice.

Wow! It smells so nice, Amir said. Everybody had their dinner and went to their rooms. Kids came to their room. Papa, you have to come to our parent-teacher meeting. I don't have time, your mommy will come. No, mommy doesn't do any work; you are a big police officer. Our friends always bring their parents who are working at good positions and then they ask what our mother does, and we feel bad. Don't say, like this, your mother is the best cook; didn't you enjoy today's dinner? Sara was shocked to hear such things from her kids; she didn't lose her calm, come here, my boys. She held their hands and told them, your momma is not just a cook, your momma is an Ayurvedic doctor, but when you two were born, your momma left her job as a doctor and became a full-time mommy to take care of you, as your father was too busy as always. Amir started laughing. Now, don't blame my kids; how much would you have earned by continuing your practice? Nowadays, nobody goes to an Ayurvedic doctor; everybody prefers an allopathic doctor; see, I am earning good enough to support you and our kids. Don't worry, boys, I will come to your parent-teacher meeting. Yeah! Papa, we love you... They pulled their hands from Sara's hand and hugged their father.

Sara, why are you angry? Every woman does this; you are not the only one. Why are you behaving like this? You insulted me in front of our kids. You are a good cook, and it's not an insult, lady. You know, I love you. I always give you money and gifts, what else do you want? You think all that a woman wants are gifts and money. Sorry, Mr. Amir, I don't need your money, all I want is respect for myself in your and my kid's eyes. Your kids love you; they can't live without you. Don't try to over-exaggerate things, said Amir. Ok, leave it. You know Sara, I got something for you. He pulled out a box from his pocket and gave it to her. Please open it; Sara, lets open it. Ok, I am sorry. Now, let's open it. Do you even feel sorry or just say it? I can say sorry a hundred times just to see you smile; now open it. She opened the box and saw a beautiful diamond ring. You bought it for me? No, for neighbors? Of course, it's for you. He put the ring on her finger. Sara smiled a little bit and said, thank you. It's very late now; I am going to sleep, said Amir, pulling blanket over his head.

Sara sat down in front of the dressing table, looking towards her reflection, tear started filling her eyes. She wiped her tears. Women who stand up for themselves are considered to be rude, and women who sacrifice everything for the family are said to be not worthy enough to get a job. When will this society understand that working or not working both women need to be respected? Respect is the basic requirement of any relationship. Without respect, love is hollow and shallow. The eyes of the partner reflect how much regard we have for each other. The unspoken language of admiration and thoughtfulness is the utmost expression of love. Definitely, I can't force you to respect me, but I refuse to be disrespected by you and anyone else. She took off her ring, put it in the box and closed it.

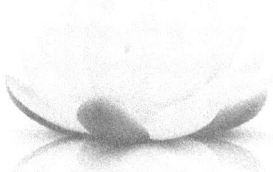

Chapter 11

Daniel went inside and showed the jailor the permission papers to meet Gabriel. Hmm. Ok, you can meet but be cautious; your brother is a bit violent, and he might harm you. Don't worry, Officer. Daniel went inside a room, a barely empty room with just a square-shaped table and two chairs. A guard stood at the entrance and told him that he had half an hour to talk to his brother.

Gabriel was continuously whispering something; he was looking down at the floor. He had clenched his fists and was repeatedly saying something inaudibly. Gabriel, my brother, please look up. See, I am here to help you. I promise to take you out of it. Gabriel slowly raised his head and looked dead into Daniel's eyes... Go away, you, monster... Just wait; let me come out of this creepy place and then I will kill you and your wife. Why do you hate me so much; what have I done? You are asking me what you have done. You were ashamed of me; you ruined my childhood... You stole everyone from me. Only Mamma used to understand me, but you took her away from me. No... I miss Mamma too, I am not ashamed of you, in fact, I am proud of you. Believe me, it's you, who taught me the real meaning of life.

Gabriel was the elder brother of Daniel. He was the first child of their parents and was loved by all. His mother would call him *jelly.* Oh, my Jelly what are you doing...? Mamma, I am drawing our family. This is Dad, you and me... My little jelly is an artist. See, such a good drawing, so don't you want to hug Mamma... Yay! Mamma. It's time to sleep now, my baby... Mamma, please sing lullaby... Sure, baby *My little Jelly wants to sleep, wants to sleep, wants to sleep... A beautiful fairy in his dream, in his dream, in his dream.... bought him gifts of love and life, love and life, love and life...* Little Gabriel slipped in the trance of soothing sleep. His Mom stood up, kissed her boy, switched off the lights and closed the door.

Honey, I am so happy that finally, our Jelly will have a younger brother, she said while rubbing her stomach. You take care of yourself; you might undergo labor at any time. A few days later, Gabriel was standing outside the hospital maternity ward, where his mother was admitted. Come on boy, don't you want to meet your Mamma and baby brother?

Gabriel went inside holding his father's finger. His mother was lying on a bed with a small, pink little baby. He tried to touch the baby, but the baby started crying. He was taken aback and tried to hide behind his father. Oh, Jelly come here, baby Momma wants to kiss you, I missed you so much, my baby. She kissed him.

One night, Gabriel woke up and listened to his mother singing... My little Danny wants to sleep, wants to sleep, wants to sleep... He went inside and started shouting, that's my lullaby you can't sing it to
him... Shhh, quiet Jelly, the baby is sleeping... Gabriel banged the door and left. He hated the mere presence of the baby. The next morning, his mother came in his room. Jelly, get up, my baby... Why did you get angry, yesterday? Momma, why were you singing my lullaby to that baby? Oh jelly, he is your brother; and see, he is so tiny, so we have to take care of him. And I love you more than anything. Ok, my baby. He hugged her mom. Momma, I wanted to tell you something. Sure, my baby, tell me. While he was about to say something, the baby started crying, Sorry, honey, let me just check why the baby is crying. Gabriel was left heartbroken. He was not ready to share his mother's love with anyone. One day while everybody was busy with their daily chores, Gabriel grabbed a knife and went inside the nursery. He placed the knife close to the baby's

abdomen, but suddenly, his Mom came and she tried to pull Gabriel away from Daniel. She got stabbed by the knife on the neck; blood started oozing out of her body. Her eyes were red, and she screamed in pain. When neighbors came rushing by and saw blood ridden body of their Mom and Gabriel holding knife. He was arrested and sent to juvenile jail.

That moment changed everything in their life. Their father who used to be a jolly man turned into a workaholic robot; that was his way to run from the harsh reality that his loving wife was murdered and that too by his juvenile son. He was angry with everyone, including himself, why he was not there; if he would have been there, he could have saved her. He instantly felt so empty and lost all the love he had for his family. Gabriel always blamed Daniel for all this; he believed that Daniel murdered his mother. He was not able to accept that he himself stabbed his mother. His mental health deteriorated, day by day and finally, he had to be admitted to a mental asylum.

Infant Daniel never knew all these things. He always longed for the love of his father. He had a nanny who took care of him, and when he was a teenager, he found all his lost love in Nancy.

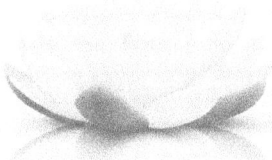

Chapter 12

*N*ancy was packing her bag. I can't live here anymore. This place is haunting me. Whether he is Ravi or Rehman, that man is very clever and dangerous. He is doing government duty and has a dual identity. I must leave. Daniel is not telling me anything, I should leave. There is no option left for me, I have to leave before Ravi tells me to do any illegal work. The phone bell rang. She kept looking at the phone, not sure whether to answer it or not. Hello....Who is this? Oh! Hi dear, I am your dear friend Ravi. I am sure you were thinking about me only, so I thought to call you up. Who are you and what do you want? You know what "What's in the name darling, call me anything which pleases you, you can call me Daniel also." Shut up and tell me why you called me. You have to do my little work before you leave for Denver. How did you know that I am going back to Denver? I know everything. Now, listen carefully. Call your boss and tell him that you want to work on the site of article 33. What is article 33? Do, as I say.

Nancy dropped the phone, placed both her hands on her face and cried loudly. Oh, God! What am I going to do, am I a puppet? How can he use me for his own benefit? Let's do it and get rid of this place. She dialed her boss's number. Hello, Boss. Hello, Nancy. How are you? I hope you are enjoying the beauty of Kashmir. Yeah, sir, actually, I wanted a few days off as I wanted to visit Denver. Sure, Sure, you can go, but sir, when I come back, can I work on the site of Article 33? There was complete silence on the other side of the phone. Then after some time, her boss responded in a dramatic tone, what is article 33? I have never heard of it. Is it some medicinal herb? Nancy understood that something was terribly wrong, but she had done what Ravi has told her to do. So, she replied in a very casual tone, oh, Sir, I may be mistaken; I desperately need a vacation. Nancy, why don't you come to New Delhi? Then, we will see how many days we could let you go. Nancy sat in despair, thinking about what this new problem was about and why his boss was calling him to New Delhi when he had agreed at first?

It was raining heavily outside. The doorbell rang. Who could be at this hour? Nancy opened the door. Daniel. Thank God! Finally, you came. I am so worried about what is going on here. Can I come in Nancy? I am all drenched in rain. I am so sorry; please, come inside. Nancy made him sit on the sofa and bought him a towel to wipe his head. Wait! I will make coffee for you. No Nancy, I don't have time for this; please, sit down. Nancy, why did you come here? Please Daniel, tell me everything. Listen, Nancy, they might be following me; I can't stay here for long, Go back to Denver. Don't you consider me as a human; you leave me whenever you decide then come back and expect me to believe you another time. Nancy, I know I don't deserve you and whatever I did to you was not fair, but believe me, every time circumstances are such that I have to go. You are telling me to go, but Ravi… Why did you talk to him? I did not; he asked me to ask about article 33 to my boss. Don't tell me you asked. Of course, I did; what other option I had? He told me he would kill you if I didn't do it. Are you sure it was Ravi? Yes, of course. Nancy, you have put your leg yourself in this dirty swamp. Do you know what is article 33? It's opium. It's the password for it, and the way your boss reacted, just confirmed that you are under the radar now. Opium??? Daniel, you again got into this stuff. No. No, Nancy, I have left all that, I can't explain you each and everything, Nancy; the less you know, the better it will be for you. Just do one thing, don't meet your boss just leave for Denver. I will meet you there. Why are you not coming? I can't leave Gabriel here all alone. I don't think he likes you. It doesn't matter; he is my brother after all. He stood up and left.

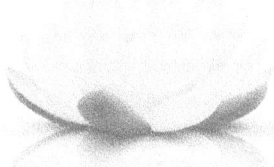

Chapter 13

The next morning, Nancy packed her bag and left for the airport with Amir and Sara. Nancy, I am going to miss you, you were the only friend I ever had, said Sara, looking at Nancy. I have to go, dear; I can't bear this anymore. I will miss you both, if you ever planned to visit Denver, do call me. Yeah, sure, Nancy. You know, people always say that whatever happens… happens for good, but sometimes, life becomes unfair and unjust, but we have to keep going. A river never stops at obstruction; instead, it makes its way out through it. She looked into Sara's eyes, I understood what you are saying, I will overcome this, don't worry. Nancy put her luggage on the trolley and entered the airport bidding goodbye to her friends. She approached for check-in; the flight took off and she reached Delhi in an hour. She had to board her connecting flight to Denver from here. She was waiting for her flight to arrive and suddenly, she was approached by an officer. Mam, can I have your ticket and passport, said an officer? Sure, you can check. The officer looked at the passport and then towards Nancy; he said, "You have to come with me, Mam." I can't. I have a flight to catch and what wrong did I do? Finally, Nancy went with the officer who made her to sit in a room for one hour. Door opened. The same officer entered with another male. Officer, how could you leave me here and go? She saw the man with the officer was her boss. Sweats started flowing from her forehead. Sir? Oh, hello Ms. Nancy, are you leaving without meeting me? No, sir; actually, it was an emergency. Oh, shut up Ms. Nancy and come with me. Fear was starting to overpower her. They both went straight to the headquarters. Come, Ms. Nancy, don't worry! Have a seat and tell me, would you like to have something cold, hot or maybe, you just want article 33? Nancy gathered her strength and said, Sir I don't know what is article 33, somebody told me to ask you this; otherwise, he will kill my husband that's why I asked you. Kill your husband? Do you really think, I am going to believe this crap? No, Sir someone called me and threatened me that if I won't ask you about article 33, they will kill Daniel. What did you just say? I mean, what is the name of Your Husband? "Daniel," Nancy Replied. Oh, no, not again. Her Boss said and placed his hands on his head. Nancy was shocked to hear that her boss knew about Daniel. How do you know him?

He is a drug peddler and he came to me many times for raw drugs which we collect for medicinal purposes. I got him arrested once. Are you working for him or maybe you are taking drugs or any information about the company to him? He had blackmailed me so many times. No, sir, I never knew he was a drug peddler and I didn't tell him anything neither he asked for it. Sir, there might be some confusion, he is in trouble. No, he is not in trouble, but he is the trouble. Nancy, I don't think you can work for our company now. I don't want to hire a drug peddler's wife. If you want to leave, you can. Sir, I am extremely sorry, but believe me, I did this just to protect my husband. You know, the moment you said you wanted to work on article 33, I knew something was wrong, and you proved my doubt by trying to escape from India. That's why, I asked my contact who is in the airport security forces to not let you go without meeting me and thankfully, he caught you. I could have easily got you arrested, but I didn't want to; you just leave. I have to give answers to MD madam about what is happening in this company. Nancy stood up from the chair, took her luggage heartbroken, left the office and went to the airport. At least, I am going to my own country, but what about Daniel; should I leave him here?

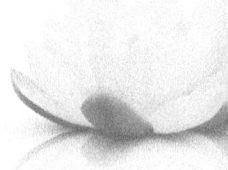

Chapter 14

Nancy was standing in the queue for boarding, when her phone rang. She answered the call; the lady on the other side introduced herself as inspector Dhami from Narcotics. Mam, you can't leave India before meeting us. But, why? I have nothing to do with narcotics. She responded in a firmer tone. Please cooperate with us, Mam. Two men in police uniforms came and asked Nancy to come with them.

She was taken to the police station and was made to sit in a cold room with two chairs and a wooden table. The lamp overhead was typically an old bulb with yellow glow. The door creaked, and a tall slim figure entered the room. Hello, Ms. Nancy, I am inspector Dhami. Nancy felt too weak to respond; instead she started crying. Don't cry, Mam, please have water. Nancy held a glass and started to drink. I have nothing to do with all this crap; please understand. Don't worry! It's just that we needed to talk. Your boss called and told us that you asked him about article 33. Inspector, I will tell you everything but please, after that, let me go back to my country. Nancy told her everything that happened in Kashmir. Okay, I want you to meet someone. Then suddenly, a man entered. Oh, hello, Ms. Nancy. Nancy raised her head to see him and the moment her eyes met his, she felt as if her whole world turned upside down. It was none other than Ravi aka Rehman. You? What are you doing here? Officer, please arrest him; he is the mastermind behind everything. Inspector Dhami smiled and said, meet him, he is Inspector Ravi. He is working as an undercover agent. Undercover agent, exclaimed Nancy? He forced me into all this shit, and you are telling me that he is an undercover agent. Don't worry, dear, we only wanted to check on your boss, but he is all clean. Nancy busted with anger you people made me a scapegoat and now, you are not allowing me to go back to my country. Oh, we are extremely sorry for all, but you have to understand that being the wife of a drug peddler isn't easy. I got this; you want to put your hands around Daniel and save some big fish, said Nancy. No, don't think so. We just want to arrest the main culprit, so please cooperate. I just want to go back to my country; to hell with your investigation. I will file a case of defamation against you all. Please understand, Nancy. We are just trying to help you, Darling. There are so many things against you; firstly, you are the wife of an infamous drug peddler. Secondly, you are working for a company which harbors the cultivation and trafficking of drugs, and most importantly, you know what all is going on. I think you have a nose for it. So, be nice and cooperate if you want to return. Nancy kept her head on the table and started crying. Ravi came closer to her and said, I promise, you will be out of here within two months or less, and I know you are not guilty. Nancy looked into his eyes and said what do you both want me to do? Please tell me clearly, no more hidden things. Inspector Dhami smiled, looking at Nancy. You don't have to do anything out of the box; just go back to Kashmir work for Edumed, just keep your senses high for anything suspicious and most importantly, motivate Daniel to confess.

But, I have been fired; how can I join again? Don't worry about it, exclaimed Ravi. After ten minutes her boss called her up and asked her if she wanted to join again or not. To which, she agreed. Dhami told Ravi to go out so that she could talk with Nancy alone. Nancy, please don't worry, we are with you; it's just a matter of fact that you were present at the wrong time at the wrong place.

I assure you that you will not be in any trouble. If Daniel could be a government witness, we could stop this drug menace and could catch the real culprit.

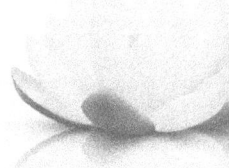

Chapter 15

It was almost 11 pm when Officer Dhami looked at her watch and exclaimed, I think we have done enough for today, so we will meet tomorrow everyone. Ravi interrupted her, but mam, we need to make a strategy on how we are going to use Nancy and how exactly she will help us. She was about to stand up from her chair when she looked towards Ravi and sat down again. Oh! Ok, so if you don't want to rest; that's fine. Meet me in my office, but first, I need a hot *chai*. Sure, Mam.

Officer Dhami sat in her comfortable chair, staring at the miniature Indian flag kept on her table. She was holding a cup of steaming hot tea. Ahh! It smells so good and refreshing. Yes, Madam, it's ginger tea. Ginger adds flavor to tea and that too in winter... it's pure bliss. Ok, Ravi, what do you want to know? Madam, I personally believe that Nancy is of no use to us. She is a foreigner and won't even understand Hindi; how will she be able to decode Kashmiri? We should let her go. Ravi, don't forget that it's the same foreigner who caught you red-handed. Nobody doubted you; it was only Nancy who suspected you. She has a nose for it.

I chose her for this mission exactly for the same reason, you doubt her. I know everyone will be thinking the same that she won't be able to understand anything, but in reality, she is far more intelligent and she somehow thinks her husband is involved, in order to protect him, she will definitely help us.

Ok, Madam just one more question, why we exposed her in front of her boss? Ravi, sometimes, I doubt why you are even in Narcotic Department. You have always been my favorite undercover agent yet sometimes, you ask such stupid questions. It's a very good saying… *whenever they doubt you, use that doubt as fuel.* Now, the boss of Edumed is alarmed and he will definitely do something, which can lead us to our main culprit. Till now, he is clean, but we have to offer bait to catch big fish. Mam, her boss now will keep an eye on every move of Nancy. Don't you think they will be more cautious around her, and now, that we have again pressurized him to get her back to work; he will definitely act more smartly. I know it very well and this will also work to our benefit as his focus will only be on her, and you will have a good chance to infiltrate.

I think, Madam, we are being somewhat harsh to Nancy. She might be feeling terrified. Officer Dhami took the miniature Indian flag in her hands and spoke. Do you know how we got freedom? We owe a lot to those heroes who sacrificed their lives so that we can breathe the air of freedom and now, my country is being paralyzed by this disease of drugs. I won't let that happen, even if it is at the cost of some Americans. What do you think about why she has not contacted the US embassy? It's because of her husband, she wants to get him out of this sh*t. So, until then we can use her. If she wants, she could get easily out of it by going to US Embassy. The reason why she avoids it is the same reason, we are using her. Most important thing is that Daniel and his brother are also somewhat involved in this scandal. She is not some random innocent lady who we are framing. She herself found out about you; and Ravi, it's somehow your flaw that she was suspicious about you. You were not able to do your job properly. If we had not confronted her, she would have exposed you in front of everyone. Our mission could have been compromised because of her.

So, now don't waste my time interrogating me; instead, get back to work and find the real culprits, not just these pawns.

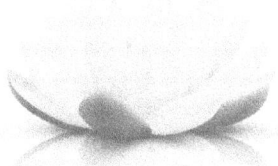

Chapter 16

*A*gain, in Kashmir, exclaimed Nancy. She was standing all alone outside the airport until she saw an old man holding a placard of her name. He was an old man with only two or three teeth, wearing a long brown pheran and a knitted cap. Nancy went straight to him. Mam, give me your luggage; I will carry it as he took her suitcase and kept it in the dickey of his car. Please have a seat, Madam. Nancy took a deep breath and sat. Madam, my name is Bashir, and I hear louder, so please bear with me. Nancy kept looking outside. She felt as if someone was following them, she looked back and saw a black Honda car, following them on every turn. Bashir stopped his car on the side of the road, as he had to attend to a phone call. That car also stopped and when Bashir drove his car, that black car followed them again. She grabbed her pocket mirror and tried to figure out who was following them, she saw a thin man with shades on his eyes. Stop the car. I said stop the car, shouted Nancy. The driver immediately applied brakes, what happened, Madam? Nancy stepped out of the car, but that car was not there. Bashir, somebody was following us. Madam, may be, somebody was following, but I am too old to notice, so please come and let's go. She sat but kept thinking only about the person who was following them. Upon reaching the guesthouse, she sat on the couch and rested for a while. She was awakened by a doorbell. When she opened the door, a masked man was standing in front of her with folded hands. She was not able to move; she could feel sweat over her face. Don't shout please, I came here to talk. She identified that voice; it was Sameer for sure. Are you Sameer? Yes, he said and knelt on his knees and asked for forgiveness.

Do you know what time is it?

I know I should have not come here at this time, but you are never alone. Please, can we just talk for one second?

Why are you covering your face?

I thought somebody might identify me and stop me from seeing you.

I feel so bad about the fact that I was not able to protect you. How did you get out of jail? They didn't find any evidence against me. But, you were caught outside my guest house. Yes, I was, but the driver quarters are also in the same area. I told them I was strolling in that area and had no intentions to hurt you.

I don't know whom to trust or not. You don't have any idea what all I have gone through, Sameer.

I came to know that you were going back to US, and I thought I would never be able to apologize to you. Thank God! You came back, but why did you come back? You have heard wrong, I had just gone to New Delhi headquarters for some work.

Nancy felt good to see Sameer, at least, she had someone to talk.

Do you want to talk over coffee, asked Nancy?

Yes, please, said Sameer smiling. Nancy came back holding two steamy mugs.

You remembered the day, I took you to my place and my mom gave you a pheran and one dress.

Yes, I do remember.

That was for my brother's wife. We were very happy as it was my elder brother Faiz's marriage after one month. We all were busy doing preparations. The Next morning, we left for Srinagar for doing some last moment shopping. We did all our shopping and then, we were heading back to our village. As we were leaving, he saw a beautiful green pheran with embellishments and motifs. He went inside the shop and asked for the cost, but we both were left with much less money. The moment we left that shop, my brother was not himself. I observed the depressed feeling on his face. Faiz, why are you upset; we have bought enough for Bhabi. It's not only about pheran Sameer, I am not worthy enough to buy anything for my wife; what kind of life is this? We came home back and the next morning, my brother was not there. I looked everywhere for him but it was all in vain. I went to Srinagar and then to that shop. I asked if he had seen my brother. Yes, your brother did come here, but.... Please, tell me where he went. Actually, he was with Hilal. Who is Hilal? Come inside and don't ever take my name in front of anybody; Hilal is believed to be a con man, maybe he works as a drug peddler. No, my brother can't be into all this. I am just telling you whatever I saw, rest you find yourself. Your brother paid for this dress and told me to give it to you. It was the same green dress. Till this day, I am looking for Hilal and my brother, but I am not able to. All I wanted was to keep you safe because this guy, Ravi, had to do something with all of this. So, I started working as a driver, to find out about the whereabouts of my brother.

I will show you the picture of my bhabi. He pulled out his wallet and showed a passport-size picture of a beautiful girl with olive eyes. Actually, this is Faiz's wallet; I have kept it as such.

She is indeed very beautiful.

So, what did you find out, asked Nancy? Nothing much, but one thing is for sure, Ravi knows more than he acts. If you already knew that Ravi had some connection, then why you used to deny it? I knew they were very powerful; I just wanted to protect you. Nancy decided not to tell anything about Ravi to Sameer. Nancy, believe me, I had nothing to do with them and at that day also, I was just trying to protect you. I had lost my brother but I didn't want to lose you. Nancy nodded in agreement. Now, tell me exactly what you were doing outside my guest room. You remember when we came back from the site, and someone was in your guestroom. Then you decided to move out of it but suddenly, you changed your plan. I just wanted to be sure that no one would bother you, but my bad luck; I got caught for no fault of mine. Nancy took a deep breath and said, still, I can't trust you. I think you should go now; it's getting late. Sameer felt disappointed, Yeah, I think I should leave. I am working in Kohinoor restaurant now; you can come anytime you want. Sure, said Nancy waving goodbye to him.

It was getting late; the black curtain of night was slowly overshadowing the golden light of dusk. Nancy stood by that window, looking out to the endless and quiet Dal Lake, sipping her freshly brewed coffee.

Chapter 17

Nancy woke up by the ringing of the phone. She answered the call half sleeping, Hello… Who is this?

No response came from the other side and the call disconnected. She was totally startled and looked at the clock; it was 3 o' clock in the morning. She could feel a shiver of terror passing through her body. She put the receiver down. Painting and sweating profusely, gathering all her strength, she looked beneath her pillow and took the torch in her hand, turned it on and walked towards the kitchen to grab a water bottle; she noticed a car outside her guest house, with headlights on. Sweat started to drop from her forehead; she switched off the torch and stood behind the curtain shivering with fear. After a few minutes, the car drove away. Oh, my God, what are all things, I am facing? I just want to go back. Should

I call Ravi? Maybe it was Ravi, keeping an eye on me. I don't want to be part of it anymore, she said crying loudly.

Golden rays of light softly touched Nancy's face; she opened her eyes and looked at the clock; it was 8 am, and she was late. Oh! No, no, I should get ready, she took bath and changed. Her driver came, and she left for her office. This time, her boss didn't want her to go to the field, so she was working in the office doing all the paperwork. She was definitely not happy with her work, but at least, this was safe. During lunch break, she went to the restaurant where Sameer was working.

Oh, my God, you have come. Yeah! So, what is special for me today on your menu?

Kashmiri wazwaan, I hope you will like it. But why don't you look good? What's the matter? Oh, nothing. Actually, I am hungry; please Sameer, bring something to eat, said Nancy hiding her feelings. Nancy sat on one of the comfortable chairs; Sameer came with wazwaan. They both sat and enjoyed it. She looked towards her watch. Oh, I must leave, I am getting late. Thanks for coming, Nancy. Hope you are alright, you can trust me. She smiled and left. Her office was within walking distance from his restaurant. She felt uneasiness in the air; she looked back to see that a black Honda car was following her; she panted heavily. It seemed as if her office was very far away; after struggling for some time, she finally reached her office.

She sat in her cabin and drank water. Why is he following me? And who is he? Should I report it to police? Oh, God, I just don't know what to do? Nancy? Nancy? Are you listening to me? She heard this voice but was not able to respond. Someone tapped on her table that she came out of her trance state.

What happened? I was trying to talk to you for about ten minutes but you were not listening. Oh, I am extremely sorry. Nancy, I need file No 41 to be completed by tomorrow morning. Ok, Faheem. Nancy took the file and started working on it. (Faheem was her new boss). The moment she finished, everybody had left, and she realized she was all alone in the office with one security guard outside. She went to Faheem's cabin and looked for anything suspicious. She opened the drawer and saw the address and number of somebody. Although it was not suspicious, she took the photograph and left the office; her cab was outside. She sat in the cab exhaling deeply. Suddenly, she felt a sense of uneasiness, she was sweating heavily. She tried to look out of the window only to find if that black Honda following her again. She wanted to bury herself in the car seat.

Upon reaching the guest house, she turned back, but there was nobody there; so she went inside. Her landline phone rang, she picked it up but nobody answered from the other side. Hello! Hello, who is this? Complete silence from the other side. I am fed up with these random calls. I just don't know who this is and why this person keeps calling me on this landline.

She sat on her recliner and suddenly remembered what she had found in the drawer of Faheem. She opened the gallery of her phone and gazed at the name, number and address written there. Mohan Salgotra, Bakshi Nagar, Jammu. She dialed the number of Inspector Dhami. Oh, Hello, Officer this is Nancy. Hello dear, how are you? Well, I am fine, but I found something in my section officers' drawer; it's actually a number of a person. I… don't know whether it will be of any help or not, but I thought I should give it to you. Yeah, sure please send me that number and keep on doing your work. Ok, thanks.

She stood up to make herself a cup of coffee. The doorbell rang; she went to the door to find Sara and Amir. Oh, my God, What a surprise! How are you? Please come inside. Oh, we are extremely sorry for coming unannounced, but I just wanted to meet you, and your number was not reachable. It's ok, darling, I was about to make coffee. We would love to have it. After a few minutes, she came out with three cups of hot coffee. Umm this aroma... it's so refreshing. Nancy, why did you come back and you didn't even inform me? Oh, nothing. I got a new assignment, and the boss didn't approve my leave. He told me to first finish the files and then go. Sara gazed into her eyes, trying to find out what she was hiding.

Amir looked into Nancy's eyes and spoke. Nancy, I need to tell you something about Gabriel and Daniel.

A sudden gush of emotions covered her; she felt as if somebody was covering her body with a rough blanket, and she was not able to see or feel anything; she stood there motionless without saying any word or making any move. Nancy, are you alright? Nancy? Sara held her arms and slightly shook it. It appeared as if Nancy woke up from a deep trance into reality. Yes... Yes, I am alright. What do you want to tell me about them? Well, Nancy, Gabriel has been deported to Denver, and it's believed that Daniel also fled, but the most suspicious thing is that why he was deported when the case was still open. I am really astonished that we were so close to finding the real mastermind behind all this and they deported Gabriel. She looked towards Amir and said what else did you find? You know, Nancy, Gabriel was becoming more and more cooperative, and he told us about one person whose name was coded as black earth. "Black Earth" what kind of name is it? I don't know, but he said it was black earth who dragged him into all this. It could be a honey trap. The woman named, as Black earth, is the one who brings the new men into all this. Daniel regularly visited the jail to meet Gabriel, and the relation between both the brothers was now getting better and better. I was shocked to know that Gabriel is being deported because he had agreed to be a government witness, but all this happened very fast, and nobody actually knew why and who did all this. May be Daniel applied the approach, or God knows what exactly happened but just in two days everything changed.

Sara took the Nancy's hand in hers and said, darling don't worry about anything now. See, Daniel and Gabriel are both now in their own country away from that black earth lady, so don't worry and try to be happy. You can come to our place whenever you want, and we will keep you updated. You just finish your work and then you will also go. Sara looked at the clock; oh, my God, Amir, we must leave, I have to prepare dinner also. Amir nodded in agreement and they both left.

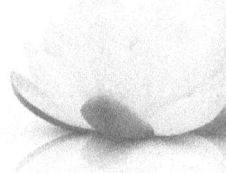

Chapter 18

Nancy was sitting in her office looking at some files; suddenly, Faheem came in and spoke. Do you finish the work I have given you? Yes boss, I have done it. Good, why don't you join me for lunch, Faheem said smiling? Nancy looked up and said yeah, sure. After he left, she thought why is he calling me for a lunch? Does he know that I was in his cabin the last day? I don't know. Oh, God, please help me. She gathered her courage and went to the office canteen where Faheem was waiting for her. Come, Miss Nancy, have a seat. Thank you, sir. What would you like to have? Sir, I will have a sandwich. Okay, sure. He ordered two sandwiches and coffee. Faheem looked towards her and said, See, I don't want to be rude to you, but I have been told by higher authorities not to be lenient; actually, I had one assistant earlier and I had been very nice to her, but she took undue advantage of this and spoiled my entire reputation, so from that day onwards, I don't want to take risks, and the way, you completed your work on time, I am really Impressed.

She was relieved to hear that Faheem was not suspecting her. Nancy thanked him for the lunch and went back to her cabin. She was working on some packaging details for saffron. At 4 o' clock, she left her office and decided not to go by the cab. So, she walked at Boulevard; cool breeze was making her hair flow with the wind; she wrapped her arms around her body, closed her eyes and took a deep breath. "Weather is too good, today. I wish everything gets normal and I get back to my place". She felt as if someone was following her, so she turned back to see that the black car was behind her. She panicked, her heart was beating very rapidly, and as soon as he reached her guest house, the car had gone. She went inside and called Inspector Dhami to report that car. Ok, ok, don't panic Ms. Nancy; have you noted the number plate? No, I haven't. Ok, no problem. If you see that car the next time, try to note its number.

"Ok. I have actually one more thing to tell you. Do you know anything about black earth, asked Nancy? "Black earth? What's it". I don't know; I thought you might know. Hey, Nancy can you please elaborate where you get that name? Actually,

Officer, one of my friends, Amir, is also in police department; he told me that because he thought it might have something to do with Daniel. Oh, ok Nancy, you are doing a very good job. She hung up the phone. I think I should not have taken Amir's name. I don't know how to correct it.

There was a knock at the door. Ms. Nancy, somebody is looking for you. Please come to the waiting hall. Who wants to meet me? She mumbled and left for the waiting hall. She saw a Caucasian man whose head was turned to the other side. Excuse me, Nancy said. The man turned her face towards her; it was Daniel.

Why are you looking for me, Daniel? What do you mean by that? We are still not divorced and most importantly, I care for you. And you know that Gabriel is getting better day by day, and now, he will be going back to Denver. So, you are going to leave with your brother? I can't leave without you. Why don't you just quit the job and come with me? I can't. I have signed a contract that I can't leave for two years. Nancy, I have already told you that it's not safe to work here. I want all the answers, Daniel; I can't leave like this. Everybody doubts me. Let me get myself out of it, and then I will come back. I tried getting out of here , but in vain. You go and take care of your brother.

Come with me please... Try and understand what I am saying. Daniel, you have always left me at times when I need you the most. So, it's nothing new... You can go wherever you want. Nancy, I have to go to Denver back as my Visa is going to get expired, so in case, you need any help just call this person; he handed her a chit, but don't ever tell anybody about this. He is the only man I can trust. I don't need it. Go away. Nancy, please take this, Nancy took that chit and placed it in her purse. Daniel hugged her and left.

There is so much I want to ask, Daniel. Maybe he is right what am I doing here; why can't I just leave? I think I should talk with Officer Dhami and see how I can leave.

The next day, Sara called her. Hello Nancy, how are you? Oh, hi Sara, I am fine. Come to my place after your office. Sara's tone was somewhat disturbed. Is everything okay asked Nancy? Yeah, everything is good, please come this evening; I will wait. Ok, sure, I will come. Nancy thought that she will tell Sara about officer Dhami, today. She kept the phone aside and started working. At 4 o' Clock, Nancy took her bag and left the office. She felt a strong urge to look back while walking on the side of the road; she saw that black car again. This time, she stopped and looked towards the driver. The car stopped, she went close to the car and knocked on the window. A handsome man stepped out of it; he came towards Nancy. Hello Nancy, how are you? How do you know my name and who are you? I am going to file a complaint at the police station against you for stalking. Oh! My apologies! I should have first introduced myself properly; my name is Edward, and I am from Denver. I used to be your senior, I hope you remember. No, I don't think I remember you. If you don't mind, can I walk with you up to your guest house? No thanks, why were you following me? Oh, I am sorry if you felt like that, but actually, I saw you at the airport; depressed. I thought you are probably in trouble. I was not sure you are Nancy or someone else. I followed you so that we could talk, but I lost you in the midway. One day, while I was returning from my office, I saw you at Boulward again, I thought about talking to you, but then again, I lost you. Luckily today, you yourself came to me. And by the way, you look beautiful. So Edward. Call me Eddie. Ok, Eddie, what are you doing here? Good question; I was waiting for this one. Actually, I am working with the red cross society, and my office is nearby only. So, I have to stay here for two years. If you have to ask me anything, you could have directly talked to me. Stalking someone is not an option. Rest, I don't want to see you again. She walked away from him and reached her guest house.

Her phone started ringing. Oh, hi Sara, where are you, Nancy? I told you to come to my place; we were waiting for you. Oh, I am so sorry, Sara. Actually, I was not feeling well, so I thought I should take a rest. Can I come tomorrow? Ok, take care of yourself, Nancy and call me if you need anything.

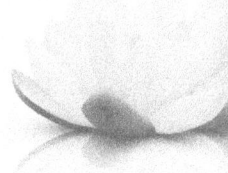

Chapter 19

The next day at work, the office was quieter than often, she went to the receptionist, Ms. Snowber, hey, is everything alright? Why is everybody so quiet? Mam, actually somebody murdered Mr. Faheem. What? Who did this? I mean how this happened? Right now, we don't know, but something is very fishy, as nobody really hated him. Police may come here for an investigation, and we have been told to cooperate.

Nancy went back to her cabin thinking of what happened and how this all happened. Officers came and called everybody in the lobby. Amir was not one of them. Everybody was taken to separate rooms for recording their statement. So, Ms. Nancy, we heard that Faheem invited you to lunch yesterday? Yes, actually he had given me some work, and I had completed it on time; I am new here so he wanted me to get comfortable with the office and the rules here. Ok, where were you last night? I left the office at 4 o'clock and then I went straight to my guest house. Mam, are you sure you went straight to your place? Of course, I am sure. No, actually I know you have been invited by officer Amir's house, but you didn't go there and even didn't inform them that you are not coming. Yes, I met somebody, so I forgot; I had to go. Ok, that's great; can you tell us whom you met? His name is Edward, and he is from the same city from where I am. Can you ask him to testify it? I don't have his number, but if I ever meet him, I will tell him. Better you tell him to testify or it will be tough for you. Are you suspecting me? Madam, we have seen your CCTV footage where you are frisking his office. I went there to search for some file; that's it. Well, take care, Mam, but don't leave the city without informing us.

Nancy went to her cabin and sat down. Snowber came in the cabin and asked her if she was fine. Yes, I am fine. I don't know what to say and what to do. Don't worry, Mam. Today, we will close the office early, so take care of yourself. We will meet tomorrow. Nancy stood up and was walking towards her guest house. She kept on turning back to see if Edward was there or not. I can't prove it without Edward. Nancy saw a police van on the other side and knew they were keeping an eye on her. She walked fast and reached her guest room. She was trying to sleep when she heard the door bell ringing. Now, who is this? She opened the door and see Edward. Edward, Thank God, you came; it was a stressful day. Really...? Are you are happy to see me? Can I come in, Nancy or we have to talk here only? Oh, I am sorry; you know, my boss has been murdered, and they are suspecting me. I told them that I was with you in the evening, but they want you to testify it. Don't worry, Nancy. I am always there for you, and I will myself go to the Police station for testifying. Thank you, Edward; I was so worried. Nancy, don't call me Edward; you can call me Eddie. What exactly you are doing here and how did you know my address? Nancy, you yourself told me that instead of stalking, I should directly contact you. So, I went to your office, but they told me what all happened there. I got your address from there only. Nancy, you got married recently, where is Daniel? We are separated, not divorced officially; we are not together. Oh, I should be saying sorry to hear that, but my heart wants to say that I am happy to hear that. What??? Nancy said in a weird tone. Do you still love him? Frankly speaking, now, I also don't know, I think he was the first person, I cared for and loved, that I never gave any other person this chance. Please don't ask me anything regarding my personal life, said Nancy.

You need to focus on yourself, don't run from things, just go deep and you will find the answer to everything. Nancy looked at him confused and spoke, how did you know this phrase? This is what my Mom used to tell me, and exactly in this tone. Oh, I have never met your mother; it just came to my mind, Thanks, Eddie for coming. Any time dear, I consider you as my friend, and I will not let anything bad happen to you.

I think I should leave now; it's getting late, and I have some important work to do. Thanks, Eddie, once again, for coming. Take care, Nancy. She came inside and sat on her sofa looking out from the window and thought should I trust him. Right now, I don't have any other option. He used to stalk me. He is more suspicious than Ravi.

Chapter 20

The next morning, when Nancy was getting ready to leave for the office, someone knocked at the door. Oh, my God, who is this at this time? She opened the door and found Sameer standing there. I am so sorry, Nancy to disturb you at this time; I know you might be getting late, but I heard about the death of Mr. Faheem. Yes, Sameer, police suspected me for all this, but thank God, Edward came to my rescue. Who is Edward? He is my old friend, who happened to be working here. Don't worry, Sameer I am fine. Yeah sure, Nancy, who do you think has murdered Faheem? I don't know, I am actually new in this office. I don't know what that person's motive could be, Let's see. Nancy, if you ever need me, you can call me anytime. Definitely, Sameer. I am getting late, I will catch you in the evening. Sure, I will be waiting for you.

Nancy entered her office and found the officers already sitting in the waiting room. Good morning, Ms. Nancy. Good morning, Officer, I hope your doubts have been cleared, now. I am afraid to say, but no mam, my doubts are still there. What do you mean? In simple words, mam, nobody came to us to verify that you were with some person, at that time. What? Edward told me that he will speak to you. No, mam, we didn't see anyone; we will find out soon; you take care of yourself. Nancy went inside her cabin, why am I getting targeted? I think I should talk to Amir. She picked up her bag and left the office. She boarded an auto and reached Amir's place. Sara opened the door, looked confused, and spoke in a whispering tone what you are doing here. What do you mean by that, Sara? Can't I come to your place? Come inside. Sara looked on both sides, pulled Nancy inside and locked the door. You know what I don't know why you killed Faheem; and you were even close to getting my husband suspended. What is wrong with you Sara? What are you talking? My husband told you about that Black Earth, and exactly the next morning, his seniors called him to ask about the Black Earth. The way, they were asking, it was clear that they were suspicious. They asked him if he had shared any departmental information with any outsider and a disciplinary committee was assigned to look into the matter. Sara, I can explain. What will you explain, Nancy? They saw on CCTV that you were in Faheem's cabin, exactly the day before his death. Sara, listen to me, I can explain. Just answer my one question, why didn't you come the day I invited you for dinner? I was with Edward. Now, who is this; Edward? He is my friend. Stop lying Nancy. Ok, you don't trust me; would you like to meet him? Yes, why not? Ok, then I will only talk to you when you will meet him.

Nancy left and went straight to her guest room, closed the gate, lied on the bed and started crying. The doorbell rang, and she stood up. She wiped her face, opened the door and saw Eddie standing at the door. Eddie, why didn't you tell the police that you were with me that day? Listen, Nancy, I told them many times, but they were not ready to listen to anything. They were just telling me why I am protecting you. Don't worry, Nancy, I am always there; I will talk with the US embassy. Eddie, if you don't mind can I call my friend here? Sure, it's your place; you can call anyone. Nancy called Sara. Sara, please come to my place; Eddie is here. Are you serious, Nancy? Because, I really don't want to waste my time. Please Sara, trust me. Ok, I will be there in ten minutes. Eddie, I was talking to my friend, I wanted to introduce you to her. Sure. Nancy, why do you want to introduce me to your friend and who is she? Eddie, she is my only friend here; she has been with me through testing times and I don't want to break her trust.

After sometime, the doorbell rang, and it was Sara. Come in, Sara. Here, meet my friend, Eddie. He stood up to greet Sara, but Sara looked disturbed. Did you call me for this? Sara, at least, be nice to Eddie. Nancy, don't ever dare to call me; we are no more friends and she left. What's the problem with your friend? I don't know why she was behaving so bizarrely. Does she know you? Why did she react this way? No, I haven't seen her. Eddie, I think you must leave now, I need some time alone, Are you sure? Please take care of yourself.

Nancy dialed the number of Officer Dhami, but nobody answered; she called her five times, but in vain, so she dialed Ravi's Number. Hey, Nancy, how are you? Please help me out; I did all this because of you people. I mean I frisked Faheem's office and now, the police are suspecting me, You people told me to do so. Nancy, we only told you to check his office, not to kill him, Oh, God, why on the Earth I would kill him? Take me out of this, Ravi. He appeared to be least interested in Nancy and said in very weird tone, ok, let me see what I can do. I will call you myself, you need not to call me and hung up.

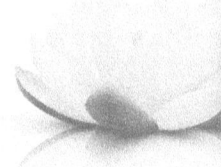

Chapter 21

Nancy woke up by a loud sound. It was raining heavily outside with lots of lightning. She stood up and closed the window which was wide open. She saw the time; it was 3 in the morning; her phone started ringing. She looked puzzled as to who it could be calling at this time. She received the call to hear a familiar voice of Eddie. Hey, Nancy sorry to disturb you at this time, but I was not able to sleep. I was just thinking about the weird behavior of your friend, and I know why she behaved like this. What? What do you know? I will tell you everything after meeting you. Eddie, I don't know what you are talking about, but she is my friend and I can't doubt her. She hung up the phone. She sat on a recliner, trying to sort out millions of things going on in her mind. I cannot doubt Sara; she has been with me through thick and thin, but why did she behave so dramatically? I think I should call

Sara. She took her phone and dialed her number. It rang and no one answered. Maybe I should listen to what Eddie has to say. She suddenly looked at the clock; it was 5 AM. Oh, how stupid I am to call her at this time, she must be asleep. Nancy lay on her bed and went back to sleep. She was awakened by someone knocking at the door. It was Sameer.

Hello, Mam, how are you? Oh, Sameer please come in. I am fine. What about you? I am very happy, today. Oh, that's great. What happened? Actually, I found some lead about my brother. Really...? That's great news. Mam, actually a shopkeeper told me that he saw Faiz yesterday in Goni Khan market. I thought I should share this with you. That's great news. Sameer, I am happy for you, but I don't know what will happen to me and when this all will end. I am so tired. If you don't mind, Mam, can you please tell me about your new friend, Edward? I don't want to hide it from you. He stalked me and then claimed to be my senior at high school, but... I don't remember him. He knows about Daniel also; he knows my address and even landline number of guest house. I was with him at the time of murder, but now, no one is believing me. Sameer listened calmly and assured her that everything will be better soon. Mam, please take care of yourself; I need to go for now, but will meet you soon. He stood and left. It was so weird of him to abruptly leave; I was not finished yet.

She went straight to the police station to enquire about Faheem's case. Amir saw her and told her that no one showed up at the police station. Amir, I even called Sara at my place when I was with Eddie. Nancy, are you out of your mind? Sara didn't tell me anything about it and I just don't understand why on the Earth I was trying to help you when all you are doing is bringing my reputation down; you spilt the information I gave you. You act suspiciously and now, you are claiming to be with a man whom nobody has ever seen or met. Nancy, the police are looking for enough evidence against you so that you could be arrested. So, please, please, if you know anything, tell me. I will try to help you, but if you don't want to tell me that, so you better be prepared for the worst. Nancy took a deep breath, stood up and left without uttering a single word.

On the way home, she got a call from Ravi. Nancy, listen to me, don't go to the guest house today. I have some secret information that you will be attacked; stay away. I can't talk more, but I will call you again, and one more thing, don't tell anybody where you are staying; even if I will ask you, don't tell me. Just stay hidden. Book any hotel or stay with your friends, but don't tell anybody about your whereabouts. Nancy hung up the phone; tear started rolling from her eyes. She stood completely frustrated in a foreign land. She went to a nearby restaurant, ordered one fresh orange juice and reminded herself of how brave she is and that she will come out of this situation as well. She covered her face with scarf, booked an auto and drove straight to Hotel Mumtaz where she booked a room.

Madam, here is your key. Nancy grabbed the key; she faked a smile and marched towards the room. Suddenly, she heard someone calling her; a chill ran down her spine. She was stopped by the hotel staff. Madam, your room is downstairs; you are going in the wrong direction. Nancy breathed heavily and tried to behave normally... Yes, yes, I know I was just roaming around. I must say your interior designer had good taste. Thank you, Madam, let me just escort you to your room. Oh, Sure.

Here, we go... This is room no. 102. If you need any help, you can call room service. Oh, thank you. Nancy locked the room and threw her handbag on the bed. Her phone rang, it was Sara, Maybe, Sara wants to talk to me, hello. Hi, Nancy, where are you? I tried calling you at the guest house, but you didn't receive it. Is everything alright? Yes, I am fine. I came for some office work. Sara, please tell me why you left the other day? Why didn't you talk with Eddie? Nancy... Nancy... I try to forget everything, but you keep on repeating. Don't you know why I left? No, please tell me. Oh, God, there was no one with you... Sara, are you out of your mind...? I was with Ed... Sara hung up the call. Nancy looked at the phone then looked up and then towards curtains; she sat on the floor and started crying. Her mascara came down with tears; she cried for hours. Finally, she stood up and looked at the mirror and started laughing. Look at yourself... You, mad girl... You ruined your life... then she tamed her hair and said you are princess... You are beautiful and again, started crying.

"Open the door"... Nancy opened her eyes, realizing that she was sleeping on the floor. She tried to get up, but her neck ached due to improper posture. There was a constant knock at the door, Open the door. Who is this? Ravi. She opened the door and saw Ravi standing at the doorway. Are you alright? What have you done to yourself? Nancy looked confused; she didn't say anything, and just kept on staring. Nancy, do you want water? There was complete silence. Ravi poured the water from a jug into a glass and gave it to her. Please drink it, Nancy held the glass and started drinking it. Are you alright, Nancy? She raised her gaze, looked directly into Ravi's eyes and said... Do I look alright? You people ruined my life, you have pushed me to the extent of becoming mad. I am not able to differentiate between what reality and what my imagination is. Calm down, Nancy. I am sorry for whatever is happening to you, but believe me, we are very close to reaching the culprit and I promise I will make sure that you reach Denver safe and sound, but for now, we don't have much time; we need to leave immediately. How did you come here? I checked your mobile location. Where am I supposed to go now...? To some place much safer, but first, wear this *burkha,* why??? Please don't ask questions; we have to leave immediately. Nancy wore a *burkha* over her jeans. Ravi fixed a fake beard and skull cap. Surely, he was the master of disguise.

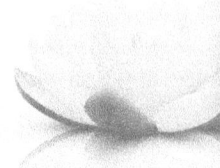

Chapter 22

It was midnight, and Amir had not returned home, Sara kept calling him again and again, but nobody answered. Sara's father-in-law knocked on her room, Sara??? Yes, Abbuji, please come in, she said while covering her head. Sara, why are you not sleeping? Abbuji, Amir is not answering my calls. Don't worry, dear, he is a cop, and you know sometimes, these Cops forget they have families too; you know as they say... "Call of the duty". He smiled; so did Sara. But, Abbuji, this case, which Amir is dealing with, somehow involves my friend Nancy too. Ahh! That American lady who came to our house?? Yes, Abbuji... I am worried about her. I think all these circumstances have taken a heavy toll on her mental health. Sara, I think you are forgetting something, What Abbuji? You are a doctor, and if you won't understand her... then who will? Sara felt a jolt of energy running through her and instantly that jolt was converted into guilt. Yes, Abbuji, she had only me in this foreign land, and I too abandoned her. What type of friend I am? Now, Sara you go to sleep and in the morning, go and meet her. Abbuji got up and started to leave. They heard the squeaking sound of brakes of car; See; Amir also came.

Amir looked tired; he put his phone on the table and sat on the sofa. Sara came in with a glass of water in her hand. I was worried; you were not receiving my calls. He drank water, put the glass on the table and looked into Sara's eyes. I don't know whom to trust; my heart says Nancy is not guilty but all the evidences are against her. One more thing, which I don't understand is why she is not reporting all this to the US embassy. Sara, you need to talk to her. Amir, I tried, I even went to her guest room, but she was not there. Yesterday, she called me to her guesthouse to meet Edward. Oh, that's great, now we can help her. If Edward will confirm that he was with her. Amir, I think Nancy is not well. I mean mentally, she needs help. What do you mean? I know she might be stressed, but right now, we have to focus on getting her out of this case. Actually, Amir, there is no such person as Edward, he is her imagination. Amir was shocked to hear that. Are you out of your mind, she seems so normal, and now, you are saying she is mentally retarded. No, no, I didn't say that; mental illness can be present in a very calm-looking person also. See Amir, it's not that she has lost her senses, but may be this stressful situation lead her to create an imaginative friend in her mind. She is having hallucinations, seeing something which is actually not there. Sara, I don't understand what you are saying. Are you sure there is no Edward? When I went there, she was introducing me to the chair. I mean there was no one sitting on the chair, but she was behaving as if she was talking with someone sitting on the chair. At first, I thought that she is making fun of me. So, I left immediately, but now, I realized that she might be having hallucinations.

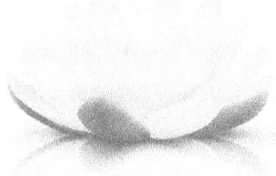

Chapter 23

Nancy and Ravi left the hotel and got in the car, already parked in front of the hotel. As soon as Nancy sat inside, she tried to pull off her veil, but Ravi stopped her. What are you doing? Why do you think I should dress like this? Nancy looked at him and said; please tell me what is going on. I want to go back to my country. See Nancy, I know what you are going through but please cooperate. I will make sure that you will return safely to your country, until then please cooperate. At least tell me where we are going. We are going to Tang Marg. I have heard about Gulmarg, but not about Tang Marg. Where is this place? It is a small town at the foothills of Gulmarg, and you will be staying there. One more thing, don't speak. I mean don't act suspiciously, because anyone will catch you as soon as you speak. Don't worry, I can understand Kashmiri, as well as Urdu, but I can't speak. You do?

Of course, before coming here, I did some work. Why are we hiding? Don't you think this will make me more suspicious in the eyes of police? Ravi looked straight on the road and felt Sorry for Nancy. I know you have been chosen as scapegoat; when you hide then only the real criminal will be at ease and will definitely make the mistake of coming out and then we will catch him. Ravi, please answer me why you told me not to tell anybody where we are, not even you?Nancy, please don't ask me questions; I will tell you everything when the time is right.

Nancy looked outside towards the trees running past her, open meadows and people walking in pherans. Everything was beautiful and peaceful except Nancy, whose heart was full of confusion. Finally, they reached a two-story wooden building. Don't utter a word, or we will be caught. Nancy nodded in agreement. Ravi talked with a person who was standing there; he took the keys, and they both went inside the house. It was an old house with minimal furniture; only one bed was there in one room and old carpets were on the floor. Nancy, you go inside that room, and I will get something to eat for us. He asked Nancy to close the door. She did as he said. Suddenly, she reached for her phone in her purse but was not able to find it. She realized that she might have left it in hotel.

After an hour, she heard a knock at the door. She went to the door and heard Ravi clearing his throat. She opened the door, and Ravi handed him a bag. You might be feeling hungry, come, let's eat something. Ravi, I left my phone at the hotel. Don't worry, it's with me. You took my phone. Ravi calmly replied, they can track you with your phone, so I switched it off and kept it with me. At least you should have told me. Ravi stopped eating and looked in her eyes. I think you are not realizing that you are a murder suspect. I am trying to save you, not only from the police but also from... From whom... Ravi, please complete the whole sentence. From BLACK EARTH. Nancy looked towards Ravi with utter disbelief. You mean that drug dealer. Oh, No, she is not any drug dealer; she runs a mafia, and I get the information that she is after you. After me? But why? I am still working on that. Ravi, please don't hide anything from me. Nancy, look, I know you are innocent and that's why I am going out of my way to help you. You should have listened to Daniel. What are you talking about? Say clearly. I mean you should have left Edumed. Nancy felt uneasiness in her body; she raised her head and looked into Ravi's eyes... How do you know this? Know what...? That Daniel asked me to leave... Nancy, can I tell you one thing...? Your curiosity got you into all this. You are not focusing on what I am telling you; instead you are focusing on who told me. Is there something I should know, Ravi? He frowned and said Ignorance is bliss and you don't understand this; the more you know, the more fatal it is for you. Ravi, you people made my life hell, and now, you are telling me to not react and just following your instructions. Nancy left that room and went straight to other room.

Hello, yes. I know, don't worry. Nobody will ever know that. We are in a safe place, and I have promised to keep her safe and I will do that. Ravi was talking to someone on phone. Nancy listened to this conversation and thought who he might be talking... Why do they want to protect me? The next day, Ravi knocked at the door. Nancy... Nancy, please open the door; we need to leave. She came out of the room. We have to leave; they came to know about our whereabouts, andwe have to leave as soon as possible. They sat in another car and left. Nancy was not uttering a single word, but the colors of Ravi's face were all gone, he was looking pale. Nancy sensed the severity of the situation and asked him, Am I supposed to ask what happened? Somebody is after us, and that's not the police. Ravi, you switched off my phone but what about your phone? You were using it also. It would have been very easy to track you. Ravi has already realized his mistake. I know, I was just informing my senior about us. Ravi, I think we should go to the police station and let them deal with it. Are you out of your mind? Nobody will believe you, and you will get killed. Do you think you are very smart? I caught you from your shoes; you were acting like a laborer with branded shoes and nice clothes. Even the dumbest person will know that you are a misfit. Ravi looked fixedly towards Nancy realizing how keenly and accurately she noted everything. You are right, Nancy; I think I have become overconfident.

Why are you helping me? What kind of question is this? Will you answer or not? I helped you because we had a deal, did you forget that…? I will protect you and you will provide us with information. So, Ms. Nancy, I am just doing my duty. Do you have any other question? Nancy didn't reply and looked out of the window as they were crossing apple orchids, herd of cattle's, flock of sheep's; she felt asleep. Nancy... Nancy, wake up; we have reached. She opened her eyes and saw that she was in another village and the car was stopped in front of another house. She stepped out of the car and followed Ravi. They went inside a house, and they were greeted by a middle-aged lady. Come inside, you might be feeling cold; please settle down.They sat on Kashmiri carpet, which was intricately weaved. She handed them the cups of khawa. The smell of cardamom instantly reminded her of Sara. What was Sara telling me about Edward? Am I day dreaming? Is there anything wrong with my brain? No, No, I have talked with Eddie. I have seen him. I don't understand what the truth is and what a mere imagination is? Don't just hold it, beta; drink it as well.

She was about to respond when she realized what Ravi has told her about speaking, so she just nodded her head. Ah, actually, *khalla* (aunt) my wife can't speak... Oh! Sorry, I didn't know it. A beautiful lady came in the room to take empty cups. Nancy looked at her face, her olive-green eyes, sharp nose, pink cheeks reminded her of someone, but she was not able to. The Older lady introduced her by saying, she is Zainab, my daughter-in-law, and Zainab, he is Saeed, your husband's friend and his wife. By the way, what is your wife's name? Ravi instantly replied, Khushboo... Her name is Khushboo. Nancy looked towards Ravi in astonishment and realized how comfortably he lies. She cant speak.

Zainab, please take Khushboo to the guest room. Go Khushboo and take a rest. Nancy went with her.

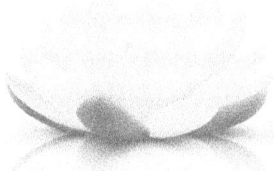

Chapter 24

It was getting late, but Sameer was still standing in front of Nancy's guest room. Sameer, what are you doing here? Sameer turned and found his colleague asking him that. I am looking for Madam. You know why you were fired, still you are here. I have seen you many times here, but I have never said anything. Now, Madam is also not here. I don't want any problem, so better you leave, please. Ok, I will leave, but first tell me where she is. I don't know, but I got a call from the office saying that Madam's mom was severely ill, so she is going back to her country. What??? Who told you this? Please leave, Sameer. I have worked with you that is why I am requesting you, otherwise, you know what I can do; so, please, leave now. Sameer took a deep breath and left. He was walking on the boulevard, her Mom is ill; I have never heard about her mom. I mean she never talks about her mom. I don't know why, but I am not able to accept that she left so abruptly without even informing me. I should have listened to her that day. I was so foolish; I talked only about myself. What was she telling me about her new friend? I don't even remember his name. I wish I could have paid heed to what she was saying. I should visit Sara... Yes, why didn't I think about it earlier? But, it's not that easy, her husband is a cop and that too, who arrested me. I will have to find a way.

Sara was cooking dinner for her kids when he heard the doorbell, Amir came early today, she thought. Hello, Mam, I am Sameer, I don't know if you know me or not, but I know you very well. Sara looked confused. Who are you and why are you wasting my time? I am Nancy Madam's driver. Sara remembered him. Oh! So, you are Sameer, who harassed my friend and now, you have the guts to come to my house. Did you just forget what my husband did to you last time? Mam, I need to talk about Nancy Madam. I think she is in problem. Sara, who is at the door, her father-in-law asked. She looked towards Sameer and replied, Abuji, it's a delivery boy from a neighboring restaurant, I have ordered something. I will wait for you tomorrow at 11.30 am at Fourteenth Avenue, Raj Bagh; be there on time, Sara said. Can't we meet nearby? Do as I say and now go from here.

Thank God, her husband is a well-known cop, and I traced his address, otherwise, I would have never reached there. I think she must know where Nancy is.

Don't just stand at the door, Sara, go to the kitchen and cook; do you want us to starve? Her mother-in-law said. She lowered her gaze and went straight to the kitchen. Why do you always keep targeting, Sara? She does everything she could do, but you are never satisfied, said Abuji. My son works day and night only for her to spend uselessly on ordering food; can't she cook? She is a useless woman, who can't take care of the kids or my son. I even saw Amir ironing his own shirt. What on Earth are you saying, Amir's mother? She is not your or your son's maid. You should be quiet, old man; you don't know how to keep a daughter-in-law. When I was young, I used to do every household chore, nowadays, women have become lazy.

I cannot argue anymore as it's useless to argue with a fool. Abuji stood up and left the room and went to the kitchen.

Sara, don't get upset by your mother-in-law's harsh words; she is an orthodox lady and she won't change her thinking. I know, Abuji, but the irony is that women themselves think they are inferior or second-class citizens. Sometimes, it hurts and my heart aches with this bias. I love cooking and taking care of my family, but that doesn't mean that I am forbidden to enjoy my life. Sara, why did you leave your job? I told you not to do so, but you didn't listen to me. Abuji, my respect should not be related to my profession; I am the mother of their grandsons and I should be respected at least. I don't know about others, but I do respect you. He put his hand on her head and left the kitchen.

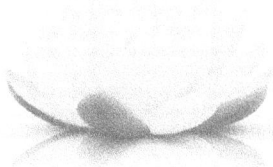

Chapter 25

Nancy sat down on the bed, thinking, what is happening to my life? It took a U-turn in just two days; now, I am a fugitive running from the cops as well the drug mafia. I don't like Ravi at all and I don't trust him, but I have no other option. He has my cell phone too. Somebody knocked at the door. She covered her face with a veil and opened the door; Ravi came inside. Don't worry everything will be fine, I know you are stressed, but this is the only way, we can save your life, so please cooperate. I want answers, but I know you won't tell me anything, so it's better to be quiet. When are you going to give me my cell phone? Sorry dear, but just forget that you even have a cell phone; I can't give it to you until we are safe. Nancy looked at him with astonishment and asked him to leave. Ok, I am going, but you remember don't speak anything.

Nancy closed the door. She was still in shock as to what has happened to her life; she needed her phone to call Sara and Eddie. Eddie.... Was he really my imagination? No, No, it can't be possible, I clearly remember his black car, his face and his voice. If he was real, why didn't he go to the police station? Only, if I could get out of this s*it, I could confirm about him; If he is my imagination, why is he not here? Or, maybe I have become conscious. One more thing, why do I feel, I have seen Zainab before; I just don't remember it. Where will Daniel be? Will he come for me, or will he just move on with his life? She remembered the day when Daniel had to go to California.

I don't want to go Nancy. You are everything to me. I can never imagine my life without you. Now, all of a sudden, you want me to go. Nancy, why don't you come with me? Daniel, I will miss you too, but you always wanted to join Stanford University. So, this is your opportunity to grab it and we will talk on the phone; we will meet when you will come home. What if our long distance doesn't work, Nancy? Daniel, we have been together for four years now, why do you think our love will be affected by 1142 miles? Nancy, if anyone else came between us, I mean what if you fell for someone else? Oh, Daniel, I love you more than anything. What is in your hand? What are you hiding, Daniel? Show me. It's nothing... C'mon, show me, baby. It was a box, wrapped in red shiny paper. Should I open it? Yeah, go ahead. Nancy was filled with excitement; she was opening her present like an eager baby. It was a crystal globe with a boy and girl dancing; it was filled with sparkle. On shaking, it appeared as if it was snowing sparkles. It's so beautiful, Daniel. I love you. I know and I love you too. Promise me, Nancy, you will always be with me, no matter what. I do... and I expect the same from you,

The last goodbye was hard, but she hoped for the better future for both of them, never she imagined that Daniel would be lost forever.

Chapter 26

Sara was sitting at the window seat of the Fourteenth Avenue Restaurant. The Sun was shining with mild pleasant warmth. River Jhelum was flowing gracefully. Houseboats were lined up. A few people were sitting on the river bank. What would you like to have Mam? Sara looked towards the waiter who was standing next to her table, holding a notepad. One cappuccino and one grilled sandwich. Sara looked at the watch; it was 11 am. Why this time is not passing? Where is Sameer? Oh, God, if anyone saw me with him, what will happen? How am I going to explain this to Amir that I went to meet this unknown man? Don't worry, Sara nothing will happen; I am here just for Nancy. She kept repeating in her mind. It's still 11.05. It seems as if time has stopped.

Can I sit here, asked Sameer? Thank God, you finally came. I have been waiting here for about half an hour? Where were you? But I think I am on time. Sit now and don't waste time standing. What would you like to have? Coffee… Sure. So, what were you telling about Nancy, asked Sara, sipping a cup of hot Cappuccino? Sameer cleared his throat. Madam, she is missing, I went to the guest house, and they told me that she went back to Denver as her mother was ill, but I don't remember her mentioning her mother ever. Even I have never heard about her mother. Something is seriously suspicious here. Her phone is also switched off.

When did you meet her last time, Sameer? I think a few days back, I went to meet her as soon as I heard about Faheem's case. She looked very depressed at that time, and yes, she mentioned her friend Eddie. That's all I know, and I am very worried about her; please tell me if you know anything. I also know this much, when I last talked to her, she seemed worried and she told me that she has gone for some office work. Sameer, you know, this Eddie who she is claiming to be her friend is just her imagination. Sameer near about spilt his coffee upon hearing this. What do you mean? She called me to her guest house to meet her new friend, but when I reached there, she was all alone there and was trying to introduce me with her imagination. She was pointing towards a chair and told me to meet Eddie. There was no one on the chair. Sameer was taken aback by this new revelation. I don't believe this; she has gone mad. No, please don't speak like this, it happens, sometimes when you are under severe stress, try to avoid reality and find peace in the imaginative world; that's what happened with Nancy.

Sameer was not able to digest this new information. I think you are mistaken; Nancy is perfectly alright and there must be any Edward. Sara figured out that it was not possible to make a layman understand this. Ok, Go then and find Edward. No, I didn't mean to disrespect you, Mam; I came here only to know about Nancy. I was thinking that if we could reach Edward, it would be of great help, but now you are saying that no Edward ever existed. I don't know what I am supposed to do. Sara covered her face with her both hands, I think we must remain alert. You can ask her company's employees who are your friends, and I will try to get some information from my husband. This is my number, don't ever call me, just message me, and I will call you myself. I don't want my marital life to be endangered.

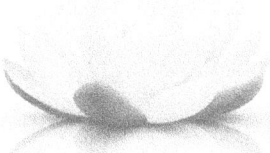

Chapter 27

It has been ten days since we eloped; I don't want to be a fugitive anymore. Are you even listening to me? Nancy asked furiously. Even, though I am not enjoying it, so it will be better for both of us to just go with the flow. Nancy, whatever I am doing is for you only. Nancy slammed the door and left. Oh, hello, Khushboo, would you like to come with me to orchids, I am getting bored here. Nancy nodded, and they both went. Zainab was a kind lady, and she used to take care of Nancy. Khushboo, I wanted to talk to you alone. I don't know whether I am right or not, but is there something wrong going on between you and your husband; I mean I can sense a clear awkwardness. Nancy felt sweat on her forehead in this winter day. She swallowed her saliva and nodded in a way to show that nothing is wrong.

May be, but you know, Khushboo, this awkwardness was there with me and my husband also. You can't talk, so my little secret will be safe with you, and also I am dying inside as I wanted to talk to someone about what's going in my mind, but I was not able to. Thank God, you came and now, I can tell you, I felt a connection with you. Can I share my story with you? Nancy nodded in agreement.

I never wanted to marry him. Actually, I was getting married to the love of my life Faiz, we were childhood sweethearts. I still remember that one phone call which changed my life; my brother-in-law called and told me that my Faiz was missing. Nancy looked astonished; she held her hand and told her to tell her in detail by the gesture of her hand. So, you are interested. I thought you will not pay any heed. Tears started flowing down her cheeks; she wiped her tears with her hands.

Everything was fixed; both Faiz and I were very happy and excited for our future. He had a blacksmith shop in his village. He was a very hardworking man and I knew he was not rich, but he was an honest man who loved me so much. My parents were not happy, at first. They rejected his proposal, but I convinced them. At last, they agreed and everything was going great. He and his younger brother went to Srinagar for doing our marriage shopping. He called me early in the morning that was the last time, I talked to him. I clearly remembered that day; he was very upset, and didn't sound like my Faiz; he was a changed man, He told me that he bought green pheran for me. Faiz, you have already bought so many dresses for me; get something for yourselves too. Zainab, it is not any ordinary pheran, it's the most beautiful thing I have ever seen, and it should be worn by the most beautiful lady; that's you. I am impressed by your taste. Zainab, can I ask you a question? Are you sure you are going to spend the rest of your life with me? I mean, I am just an ordinary blacksmith. What are you talking about Faiz, from where the money came? I love you and I think this is more than enough for me to live with you. Zainab, I want to see you in that green pheran before I go… Before you go? Before you go, where? Are you planning to leave me...? Tell me clearly what you are about to do. Nothing, I am always there for you Zainab. Don't worry, I won't leave you. Faiz, everything is decided, and my parents are also happy now. Please tell me clearly if anything is bothering you. We both will sort it out. Complete silence was there. At least, say something, Zainab heard sobbing, are you crying, Faiz? No, No. Please Faiz tell me, what happened? Faiz broke down, I am sorry, Zainab. I think I messed it all. They won't leave me. Who? Faiz, what happened? Ok, Zainab, listen to me, if I didn't come back, please don't wait for me to get married. Why won't you come? Who is after you?

Black Earth. Faiz whispered. We will go to the police; don't worry, Faiz. No, I can't trust anyone. I love you always, and he hung up the phone. Nancy could feel her heart pounding, Black earth, again. Should I tell this to Ravi? No, I think I should wait. Could she be talking about Sameer's brother and that pheran, which her mother gave me? Something is seriously wrong here. What had happened to Sameer's brother? Is her brother even alive?

Then my parents got me married to Danish, but my bad luck; he too died after two months of our marriage. Now, I don't want to get married again. I am ok living with my mother-in-law, she is a good lady. My heart belongs only to Faiz, so marrying someone without your heart is also a bluff.

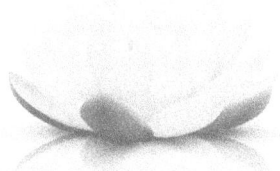

Chapter 28

Nancy was totally astonished by the fact she learned that day. How am I going to confirm that she was talking about Sameer's brother? I have to find a way. Ravi was standing at the door. What are you thinking Nancy...? I mean, Khushboo. He closed the door behind him. Nancy, we have to stay here for a few more days, and then we are free to go. This time Nancy responded with a smile on her face. Sure, you take your time, and when things get better, we will leave. Ravi looked suspiciously towards Nancy. Are you alright? I thought you would shout, that's why, I closed the door, but you seem to have changed. I think the beauty of this village made you fall in love with it. Yeah, and I like the peace and serenity here, which I don't get in the city.

Ravi stood up and left. He came out of the house, sat in his car and drove towards the nearby town which was *Magam.* He stopped his car in front of a two-storied building and waited in his car. He saw a white Hyundai car stopped in the parking area and a fair man stepped out of the car, adjusted his tie and looked here and there. Here, he is, exclaimed Ravi. Hello, Dr. Irfan, how are you? What are you doing here? You know I can be in trouble if anybody saw us. Oh! Doctor *Saab,* I had pain in my tooth, that's why I came to visit you. Ravi came closer to Dr. Irfan and said, don't create a scene over here; let's talk in your clinic and act normally. Dr. Irfan frowned and went straight to his clinic. You have renovated your clinic; it looks much better now. What on earth are you doing here and do you really think just by adding a beard and copying accent, no one can recognize who you are? I identified you in one glance. Oh, my dear *Dr. Saab*, you recognized me because you already knew that I was waiting for you. I told your assistant to inform you. Ok, now tell me why you are here.

Dr. Saab, you have helped me earlier, but this time, I need your help again. I need you to take that chip out from my tooth that you had earlier inserted. Dr. looked puzzled. Are you sure? Last time, you pointed a gun at my head when I rejected your order, and now, you are telling me to pull it out. Don't ask questions and just do what I am telling you to do. He placed a patient drape on him and after examining his mouth, started working on his lower first molar. He took a crown removal forceps and carefully removed his crown. He placed an inverted cone bur and put it in the air rotor. The sound of air rotor filled the whole clinic. He started drilling, removing the white-colored filling. He removed the debris with an air sprayer and with the help of forceps extracted a red-colored chip from his tooth. He then filled the crown portion with permanent restorative material and placed the crown upon it. Now, it's done… I hope we will not meet again. Ravi got up from the dental chair, took his chip and securely placed it in a plastic container. Thank you, Dr. Saab, I wish I have a stun gun from the movie, Men in Black, so I can erase your memory. Don't worry, mister, I don't want to get involved in anything; as a matter of fact, I don't even know your name. I have only seen you in different avatars. Ravi smiled and exited his clinic.

I don't know whether I have done wrong or right, but at least I should know what information is stored in my teeth. As per departmental orders, this should never be removed and only at the time of emergency should it be removed, and this is an emergency. Ravi recalled the day when Officer Dhami told him about this chip.

Good morning, Officer Dhami. Very Good morning, Officer. Come, have a seat. I was about to call you.

Actually, I am going to assign a very important task to you. You performed very well in your last task. This is a piece of highly confidential information, which should not go out of our department. Sure Mam, I will keep it in a safe place. No, No. It should always be with you, you can't trust anyone. You should embed it in your teeth; that way no one will ever know, and the information will always be safe. If you don't mind Madam, can I know what is in it? No Officer, even I don't know what is in it. Your name has been recommended by my seniors. Sure Madam, I will keep it safe more than my life. Now go and find a dentist who will agree to do this and will never open his mouth. Don't worry, Mam, I know where to go.

He went straight to Magam, a town on the outskirts of the city. I have seen a new dental clinic yesterday here, and that will be perfect for me. Ah, here it is... Dr. Irfan's Dental health care Clinic; he was greeted by a receptionist. Hello Sir, do you have any prior appointment? No, I don't have, it's an emergency, so I didn't have time to make an appointment. No problem, Sir, we were expecting one of our patients, but I think they might be late, so you can meet Dr. Irfan now. Oh, thank you. He went inside and saw a young fresh face. Please get yourself comfortable and tell me what your chief complaint is; I mean what bought you here. Ravi showed him the chip and told him to embed it in his teeth. What nonsense is this and what is this chip? Dr. Saab, you only do what you are supposed to do. Get out of my clinic; I don't want any scene here. I want you to be out of my clinic now.

I thought you will be intelligent enough to understand what I can do, but it's OK. I think you don't understand my language, but you will definitely understand my friend's language. He took out his gun and aimed directly at the Doctor's head. Dr. Irfan was so shocked that he could barely move. Please put it down, I will do it.

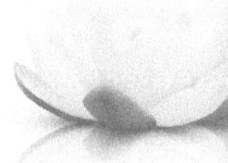

Chapter 29

Mommy, please pack my lunch. Here you go my baby, take care and study well. Sara, I will be late, so please get the kids from school. Yes, Sure Amir. Her phone beeped, she took her phone and saw a message and kept it on one side. Sara, where is my morning tea? Coming, Mummy. She ran inside the room with a cup of tea and flat slices of bread. Why are you so lost today, Sara? Nothing, Mummy, I will talk to you later, as I have lots of work to do in the kitchen. She ran into the kitchen and started cleaning the counters. She then read that message again. A wave of uneasiness covered her. Her heart started beating faster than usual. She went into her room and locked the door. She dialed Sameer's number and asked him to meet her.

She packed her bag with few clothes and a file of documents and slowly sneaked out of her home. She ran out of the main gate and ran towards the taxi stand. She sat in the taxi and left. How is this even possible? I should hurry. What do my children do when they will come to know that their mom eloped? I am sorry my babies, but Mommy is left with no option. I have to correct many things.

Sameer reached 14th Avenue and went straight to the seat where Sara had met him earlier. I think she might be late. Why did she call me in hurry? Oh, Lord, is Nancy safe? Please God, take care of her. Sir, what would you like to order? Sameer looked confused while looking at the menu. He pretended to read and then said. I want water, I am waiting for someone. I will order when my friend will come. OK, sir. The waiter left. Sameer took a sigh of relief, ordering in these modern restaurants is quite difficult compared to our traditional hotels. The waiter came after an hour. Sir, do you need to order anything? It's been an hour and the person you are waiting for has not turned up. Sameer looked over his phone and thought, she told me not to call, what am I supposed to do now? I can't afford this restaurant, better for me to leave. I will leave; I think my friend forgot to come. The waiter looked doubtful. Sameer started moving towards the gate when he saw Amir coming into the restaurant. Sameer pretended to be on phone, but Amir saw him. He snatched his phone, whom are you talking to with a switched-off phone? Sameer was frightened, why did you snatch my phone? Come with me, I will tell you everything.

Sameer followed Amir to his car in the parking and they both sat in. Tell me where my wife is. I don't know; how am I supposed to know where your wife is? Don't fool me, you were the last person she talked to and messaged you to meet here? Why were you meeting and for how long is this going on? You are the same guy whom I arrested because you were bothering Nancy. Answer me you idiot; don't stare towards me like a dumb person. Answer me you, damn… Amir placed his fist on the steering.

There was nothing wrong between me and Sara; we were just concerned about Nancy. It is the only reason we met. Nothing more! We have met only once before and this is the second time, she asked me to meet but she didn't turn up. I have been waiting for her for an hour.

Amir looked dissatisfied; do you think I am going to buy this story? Sara has eloped from home, she had taken her clothes and documents. The only thing, I found in our room was this phone and your last call.

I am a cop working on Nancy's matter. I can give her all the information, she needed. Why would she meet you? Tell me where my wife is. I don't want to make this issue public, that's why I am not taking you to the police station.

Sameer looked helpless; I swear, I am telling truth. I was also waiting for her. She messaged me to meet her as soon as possible. I thought she might be having any information. I know you are worried, but believe me, you are wasting your time with me, I have nothing to do with your wife. If I had to run away with her, why I will be waiting here? Or why would she leave her mobile phone at home? I am not a person of enough knowledge, but.......... He paused for a second.... But maybe she knew something regarding Nancy, which somebody didn't want her to know and had now kidnapped her.

No, it's clearly seen in CCTV, that she left on her own and the only call she did was to you.

Please believe me, go to the nearest taxi stand or auto stand and enquire about her, before it's too late.

I am leaving you for now, but my eyes are always on you. Now, get off my car and don't discuss it with anybody.

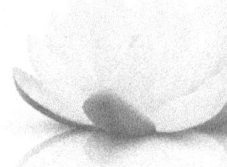

Chapter 30

Ravi was sitting in his car and staring towards the chip. Am I doing the right thing? I don't just want to be a keeper of the secret, I should also know it. I have been loyal to my department, but something somewhere is not alright, that I know for sure, so let me first know what is in it. It was a small dark red-colored chip, with a size of a rice grain. How am I supposed to know what is in it? I don't have an appropriate armamentarium. Ah, I know who can help me; yes, I can trust him. He drove his car to another nearby town, *Pattan*. After twenty-six minutes, he reached his destination, a small town with numerous shops, he parked his car in front of a blacksmith's shop, came out of his car and walked inside.

How can I help you, said the man inside the shop? I want to meet Imran. He is inside, the man said pointing towards another room within the shop. He went inside the room; it was a dark room with a zero-candle red-colored bulb, giving the whole room an X-ray room-type appearance. Come in Sir, what are you doing in the doorway? I have an urgent piece of work with you... I know; I know.... you only remember me when you have any *urgent piece of work,* smirked Imran. Tell me where are you? I am not able to see you. Imran laughed and came out of the adjacent room. So, tell me how can I help you?

Ravi came directly to the point; I need you to decode this chip for me. I need every detail of it. I don't do illegal work now, I am a traditional photographer, and capturing wedding photographs is my business, nothing more than that. Stop this nonsense, who do you think you are fooling? It's a digital world nowadays, and you are still stuck in the era of negative development of photographs. Imran laughed again and said, I am just kidding, you have saved me many times; you know my passion for hacking. I enjoy it and I know you also believe that I am the best in my profession. Yes, I do. Now, please tell me what is in it. Ok, please sit on this chair while I will do my business. Do you want some tea or coffee? No. Nothing, just be quick.

Ravi sat on a plastic chair, what might be in it? Am I a traitor; no, no, I am not a traitor. I just want to know what I am protecting. I will go to that dentist again to put it back, after I will gain the information. Ravi's self-talking was interrupted by hysterical laugh of Imran. Dude, you must be out of your mind; what did you want to decode from this? Ravi ran towards him. Why are you laughing? What is in this? Dude, you have been fooled; there is nothing in this chip. It is actually a GPS tracker. Ravi was not able to believe it. A GPS tracker?? I was protecting a GPS tracker. No, it means someone keeps tracking of your every movement, corrected Imran. Ravi took the chip and left. Imran yelled from back, you can come anytime to me; I owe you a lot.

Ravi closed the car doors and placed his hands on the steering. They know where we are, and they can come anytime. I must save Nancy; she is innocent and being framed; she is used as scapegoat like me to save the big fish, but first let me take her to a safe place.

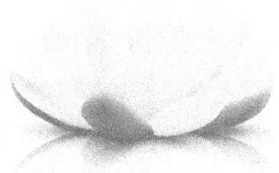

Chapter 31

How should I talk with Zainab? Ravi has clearly instructed me not to speak, otherwise, we will be in trouble. Should I write? Maybe she understands English, No, Nancy you are in their country, so I understand their language, but it doesn't necessarily mean that they will understand mine. What should I do? Ravi came inside the room without knocking. His face looked pale and he was sweating profusely. Do you want water, said Nancy holding a bottle of water? He grabbed it and finished the whole bottle in one go. Oh, you might be very thirsty, smiled Nancy. We must leave? Nancy looked confused. Now? You told me yesterday that we have to stay here for a few more days, and now, you are telling me to leave. Nancy, we are in trouble. I don't have time to explain this to you right now. Just pack your belongings and we must leave.

Nancy did what Ravi told her to do. *Khala*........
Khala.... (Aunt) We are leaving, shouted Ravi. What happened? Is everything alright? Why are you in hurry? No, *Khala,* her father is seriously ill and wants to meet her daughter, we must leave quickly. Nancy looked towards Ravi in disbelief. This man is such a big liar, not even sparing my father. Nancy nodded in agreement. At least eat something. No, Khala, we must leave now. Aunt hugged Nancy and gave her 2000 rupees. It's a culture to give money to new brides or babies when they are leaving. Nancy resisted at first, but then took it. Nancy hugged Zainab and left.

Ravi drove the car as fast as he could. Nancy looked towards him. Please slow down, we might die. Yes, this is the point, if I drive fast, we might die, but if I drive slowly, we will definitely die. It's of no use talking to you. Nancy, I swear, I will tell you everything, but first we reach a safe place. Nancy closed her eyes, as he was driving very fast. Nancy remembered how sometimes, Daniel used to drive fast to frighten Nancy. Daniel, stop driving fast; you know I don't like it. Its speed, its thrill.... responded Daniel. Surely, it can kill... Slow it down, please. Don't worry, Nancy, I will always do whatever pleases you; he slowed down his car, and she smiled an ear-to-ear smile....

Ravi looked towards her. Why the hell are you smiling? Does it all seem exciting to you; running from cops and changing get-ups? Nancy realized that she was not with Daniel, but with Ravi and they were running for their lives. Where are we going? And even this time, do I have to play dumb? Ravi paused for a moment. No, not at all, this time, there will be nobody greeting us. These people were so nice to us, Ravi, but you have lied to them as well. For them you are some Saeed. I will tell you everything, I promise, but let's just reach our destination, i.e *Pattan.*

After one hour's drive through meadows, they finally reached *Pattan.* He parked his car in front of a lonely house in the center of a meadow. It was already dusk. Nancy stepped out of the car and followed Ravi. He opened the lock and went inside. It was a nice house. It had three rooms with beds, one kitchen and attached bathrooms with two rooms. Nancy, would you like to have some coffee? I would love to, but from where you will get coffee? I have kept everything. Nancy smiled in a taunting way. I am not kidding... He went inside the kitchen and grabbed a Nescafe coffee powder and showed it to Nancy. Freshly brewed coffee for you, Madam. Nancy smelled the coffee mug... I was craving for this aroma. So, Nancy, do you have any idea why are we running? Nancy took a sip of coffee. Yes, because my life is in danger and the police suspect me of killing Faheem. Ok, then why am I helping you? I mean I am also a cop, so why am I going next level to save you? Nancy looked confused. I don't know, maybe you think I am innocent. There is more to it, we are not running from the cops, we are running from the Black Earth. Black Earth... Why is she after me? Nancy, you are a scapegoat, just like me... Scapegoat, just like you...? Explain, please. I am not able to understand a single word. Ok, I tell you from starting. So, your husband Daniel and I are good friends. Nancy got up from her chair. Stop right here, please stop. Don't bring my husband into all this; he told me to stay away from you and now, you are telling me that you and Daniel are good friends. Nancy, please calm down, there is so much more you need to know, but first, please listen to what I am saying. If you will keep interrupting, I won't be able to speak and I think you have every right to know the truth.

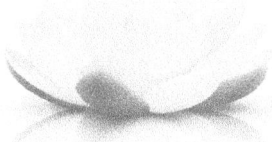

Chapter 32

She sat down and started moving her legs, I won't stop you now, you speak, but remember one thing, I am not a fool, and I know how big liar you are. He looked up and then gave a tiring look to her. I am a person who never talks about myself, but today, I am talking; there might be some reason, so please listen. Consider it as I am telling you a story, but please listen. Nancy nodded. Okay, anyways I don't have anything to do with it; I will listen to your crap. Thank you, Nancy. So, basically, my name is Saeed. Nancy looked in disbelief but didn't say anything. Yes, my name is not Ravi, my name is Saeed, and I am from Kashmir; the place where we were staying was my friend's place. We were childhood friends. Nancy didn't look contented by what he was saying. Stop stereotyping me, I know what you are thinking; I don't look like Kashmiri, definitely, most of the Kashmiris are tall, fair and have a sharp roman nose, and I am short-heighted with a somewhat dusky appearance. The point is that there are exceptions everywhere, not all Kashmiris are fair-skinned, and I don't copy accents. I act as if I am copying, when I don't want anyone to know that I am Kashmiri. When I was working on your company's field, I acted deaf and dumb, because that was the easiest way, no one will know I am Kashmiri. I accept, I didn't work on my clothes, and you got suspicious.

I worked for the Narcotics department secret services. Our mission was to bust any drug scandals and stop the spread of the drug menace, in order to keep my identity secret, my seniors gave me a new name, and you know what that is…. Nancy responded, "Ravi". Yes, exactly, that's my current name. So, the company you are working with i.e, Edumed came under our suspicion as within only one year of launching, Edumed spread to foreign lands and also the high-ranking employees of the company were foreigners. This company is Delhi based, and its branches are in almost every state of India. Being Kashmiri, I was told to extract information from here, I thought acting deaf and dumb would help; most importantly, people will think I am not able to listen; even if they will speak in the local language, I will not be able to understand. One year ago, when I came here and worked in the fields, I noticed a foreigner working on the fields too. I got suspicious of him and one day, I decided to go to Edumed's main office for getting some information. Before I could get there, I saw a few people beating a man. I had my face covered with a monkey cap, so I went there and saved that man; to my surprise, it was the same foreigner. I took him to a nearby chemist's shop and after doing first aid, we were walking back. Thank you, I owe you a lot man. No worries. May I know who those people were and why they were beating you? They were goons; I can't tell you anymore. Okay, no problem; in which hotel are you staying? Please tell me, I will drop you there. Oh, No, No, I will go myself, it's not far from here. I pulled off my monkey cap. You??? I have seen you somewhere. Yes, I work in the same field where you work, but I think you were deaf and dumb. How can you speak? Leave that; first tell me, what are you doing here? I think you are working illegally here. I don't have money to go back, so I am just working to get money for tickets. What is your name? My name is Daniel, and I am from the United States of America. If you wish I can give you the money. You work in fields, how will you give me money? Don't worry about that. If I can speak, I can also send you back to your country. So, tell me on which date you want to go. No, I can't go, not before I find my brother. Your brother is here. Yes, I am sure my brother is working with this company only. He had joined five years back. Someone gave me tip, so I came here without telling my wife, because I never knew I had an elder brother; it was only a few months back when my father told me about him before dying, so I started searching him; finally, I came to know that he is here. It was difficult for me to explain all this to my wife, and I didn't want to involve her in all this. But your wife must be worried about you. I know, but who knows if I will be alive to reach back or not, so she will think of me as a betrayer and will move on in her life. So, did you find anything about your brother? Yes, I found that he was managing the Delhi branch for five years, and then he was transferred to Kashmir; after that, nobody knew where he was. He was last seen in Kashmir. So, today, I thought of breaking into the office and getting access to computers or any files which would help me find my brother. As I was going into the office, these goons attacked me.

Now you tell me who are you and why are you acting as deaf and dumb? Well, because I am also looking for someone; and from now onwards, I will look for your brother too. Daniel looked towards him with a ray of hope in his eyes. But Daniel, you need to promise me that you are not going to tell anybody about me. My lips are zipped; don't worry, dude.

We both acted as drug peddlers, to know more about their business. Daniel even went to your current boss for raw drugs, but he got him arrested. We gained a lot of information while doing this. One day, he came to me after you joined here. What happened, Daniel; you looked stressed? Yes, in fact I am; I told you about my wife, she has joined this company. I saw her today in the field. Why don't you tell her to go back? I know her very well, she won't listen to me, but I will try. Tell her that she is not safe here. He told me that he had called you to meet him at 10 pm in the alley; it was the same point where we used to meet drug dealers. I told him that he did wrong calling you there, but he said you won't notice anything; but again, you caught me. As a part of my mission, I acted as a small drug peddler to catch the big fish. While I was doing my work, you saw me, and then you got hung over me. One fine day, you confronted me; I tried to act as I did not understand you, but you were so adamant that I had to intimidate you, and the worst part was when you were confronting me. My seniors heard our entire conversation as I was wearing headphones and had a little transistor attached on my shirt. And, since that moment only, my seniors ordered me to use you as bait, as you had a nose for digging up old graves. One day, Officer Dhami got information from her informer that Gabrial was hiding in the Nishat area of Srinagar. I told this to Daniel, but before we could reach there, Officer Dhami reached there and got him arrested. Daniel then began to fight a legal battle to get Gabrial out of the jail.

Can I stop you for a moment please, requested Nancy. Just answer this question, why didn't he tell me the truth? Why was he always in a hurry? Nancy, he never wanted anyone to know you were his wife because he had enough enemies here, as he knew much more about Edumed than he should.

But the most mysterious thing happened when Gabriel came to your house out of nowhere. How did he found about you and the exact position where you were even after getting arrested? We were not able to get any information out of him, as his mental condition was not alright. When his mental condition improved, they deported both Daniel and Gabriel. Daniel came to me and told me about that. I was shocked to hear that, but he promised me to ask Gabriel about his whereabouts and everything about Black Earth and then tell me, but in return, he asked me a favor… To keep you safe…

No, it can't be true; I don't believe you; he can never trust you. I think you forgot that it was only you who asked me to call my boss and tell him about article 33. Yes, yes, I know, I didn't have any other option; my seniors were all there when I called you. Though I had seen you at the Srinagar airport when you were leaving, I reported of having not seen you, but my Senior Officer Dhami caught you and I had to come to Delhi. You are a professional liar. I am not going to trust you, if you were Daniel's friend, why he never mentioned you? You don't trust me? No, I can't. Ok, do you remember that Daniel gave you a chit and told you to call this number when you are in need? Go and check whose number is this? Nancy got up and started looking in her purse, she took out a piece of paper which she had kept in the front column of her purse, and she saw the number 94190234. She came inside and said, what is your number? He smiled and said 94190234. Nancy was stupefied. I don't believe this; you mean Daniel asked you to take care of me, and all this while I thought he never cared about me. No, Nancy, he loved you so much, but the quest of finding his brother took a heavy toll on his life; but yes, at least he got his brother and now, I have to safely send you to him.

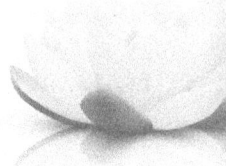

Chapter 33

Your seniors used me as a human shield? In a way, yes. Who killed Faheem, then? Nancy, I don't know who killed Faheem, but the person who killed him is the same who is after you. What I feel is that they want to divert the focus from the main culprit to you, so the spotlight shifts to you, and that person can live freely and you get to pay for their deeds. You told me that you are also used as a scapegoat, what did you mean by that? My seniors are monitoring my movement; they even fitted a GPS tracker in my teeth. They lied to me that it was an important chip of the department which contained secret information, which shouldn't be shared with anyone. So, it clearly shows there is some loophole in my department. I am not able to figure out why they are tracking me. Nancy thought for some time, can you tell me exactly when you got this chip implanted? I think about one year ago. You mean, the same time, when you were working with Daniel, right? Yeah, near about that time. So, it's simple, they didn't want to track you, they wanted to track him. He didn't seem pleased by Nancy's speculation. No, I didn't think so, Nancy. She started biting her nails; can you please at least tell me, who killed Faheem? Do you have any idea? Or was it your department after it, to frame me? No Nancy, Faheem was an ordinary employee; he was a common man, with no important links or any sort of indulgence in illegal matters. He was a clean man; his death has raised many questions. Nancy looked dissatisfied with the answers. Ok, Nancy, tell me about that man... What was his name. Edward? Nancy was reluctant to answer the question. Nancy, we don't have much time, at least if we will tell everything to each other, we would be able to get out of this situation, but if we keep on hiding facts, we both will be in grave danger. Nancy hesitated first and then said, he was no one, Edward doesn't exist. His jaw dropped,

You mean, you lied to everyone, but why?? Why did you even lie? Tell me Nancy, did you? No, I can never kill anyone and why would I harm him? He was a very good human. Can you please elaborate me then why you lied about Edward? I didn't lie. He looked frustrated... Unbelievable; Nancy, first you told me that Edward doesn't exist and now, you are telling me you are not lying; I am not understanding a single word, please clarify. Nancy hung his head, as if in shame. Then she gathered her strength and said, well my mental condition was not stable, I was stressed, and maybe that's why I imagined a friend. He was startled. I don't want to sound rude, Nancy, but please it's not the time for jokes. You were so confident about Edward that day, and today, he is just an imaginary friend. I don't believe this. Nancy got steamed up, you think I am joking? I know no one will trust me, that's why I was hesitant to tell you all this, but you said that you wanted to know. He realized his mistake. Ok, Nancy, I am not a counselor or therapist, but consider me one and tell me from the beginning. Are you sure you want to listen? Yes, definitely, please begin. It all began when I came back from the airport; I saw a black car following my cab, so I told the driver to look, but he said no one is following us, and then I started seeing that car in front of my guest house at an odd time. After that, I received calls at 3 am on the landline, but nobody ever spoke from another side. The day, Faheem got killed, my friend Sara had invited me to her house. As soon as I left the office, I saw that car following me again. I pulled myself up to confront the driver, and asked him to come out. To my surprise, he was an American, who worked with Red Cross. He said he was my high school senior and wanted to see if I am fine; I told him not to follow me, so Sara's invitation skipped out of my mind.

Next day, everyone suspected me of killing Faheem, Even Sara didn't trust me. Luckily Edward came to my guesthouse and told me that he will go to the police station and will tell everyone that you were with me, but he never went. Nancy, sorry for stopping you, but how does it prove that he doesn't exist? When he was at my guest house, I called Sara at my place to meet Edward, but when I tried to introduce her to him, she left the guest house and got angry. I never understood what happened, but she called me other day and told me that there was no one; I was imagining him, that explained the fact that why he never went to police. Well, well, I have just one question for you Nancy; if Edward was your imagination, then did you saw him again? I mean when we were at khala's place, did you ever see him? If he is your imagination then he could come anywhere, right? No, I never saw him again, but the reason can be that I realized that he is not real and my brain stopped playing with me. He smiled, Nancy, do you really think, it's so easy to control your brain? It requires psychiatrists, counselor and much more things, and you are saying, your condition got cured just by realizing that you have imagined him. Sara is a doctor; she knows much more about mental issues than we do. Accepted, but Nancy, it's hard for me to believe. I understand that you were facing a tough time, but having an imaginary friend who stalked you and called you up at 3 am; what kind of friend was this? By the way, why was Sara angry with you, because you had an imaginary friend? Nancy responded angrily. You tell me one thing, when I told you about the Black Earth, why did you leak information to Amir's seniors? She was upset with me because of this and she thought I am lying. Oh, wait, wait, wait... Now, you are telling me that we leaked the information that you told us about Black Earth, after hearing from Amir. Yes, that's what I am saying. He started laughing... It's not possible, we are not some kindergarten kids that we tell him what we heard. Then tell me how did he know? I had told someone. He took a long pause. Placing his hands on his forehead, how can I not see it? Not see, what? Nancy, I got all my answers. I knew who the Black Earth is and why there was a GPS tracker in my tooth? Nancy waited patiently for his answer, but he kept repeating, how can I be such a fool? Nancy finally lost her cool. Now tell me, who Black Earth is. Nancy, you gave information to Officer Dhami about black Earth as well as Faheem. Yes, so what? She is herself the Black Earth; she asked me to put this chip in my teeth and she killed Faheem, because she knew you frisked his office. It will be easy to suspect you, when you mentioned the Black Earth. She got worried and threatened Amir.

Nancy asked in a worried tone, but now, you have removed GPS tracker from your mouth; she will know that and will start looking for us. Nancy, I have not only killed time in my department, but I have also learnt so much. My tracker is with someone I trust and is within that village only. You remember the first position where we were hiding, I talked to her only, and the next day, she told me the cops have known our location. I don't know why, but she wanted me to be out of that village… She could have easily attacked us when we were at your khala's place. Maybe she wanted to get rid of me or you for some time and then she could easily attack us; now no one will believe a fugitive.

Chapter 34

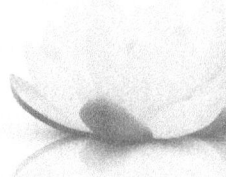

"Why are you late, Sameer? We have customers to attend, go inside the kitchen and start preparing mutton. Sameer went inside the kitchen and was totally out of focus. First, Nancy went missing and now, this Sara, what is happening? I don't want them to have the same fate as Faiz. Something somewhere is common between all these three missings; all of them went by themselves; no trace; nothing. Did Sara know something and want to tell me? But why didn't she call her husband? She called me to meet, packed her bag and left. Something is not right. She even left her phone at home… Maybe she forgot to carry it. It can be a possibility that someone was telling her to do so.

You haven't yet started preparing mutton; it was my mistake that I gave you a job here. I am sorry, Sir, but I have to go. You have to go?? Where? Who will prepare mutton for customers? Sir, he will do it, he said pointing towards the other chef and left... Don't you ever dare to come back; the doors to this restaurant have been closed for you... I am sorry, Sir, he said while removing his apron and left.

Sameer boarded an auto and went straight to Dalgate police station. He went inside and asked for Officer Amir. The constable there told him that he had been transferred to Pattan police station. He boarded a taxi and went straight to the police station and then to Amir's cabin. May I come in Sir? You? You came again? So, finally, you want to say the truth?... Officer, first of all, please understand that I have no role in your wife's missing case; I came here only to tell you something. Sir, don't you think the pattern of Nancy and Sara's missing are very similar? What do you mean?... See, both Sara and Nancy went with their bags packed and went on their own?... So, what's the point? My point is that maybe, someone is telling them to do so. And, why would anybody tell them to do so and why would they follow? Maybe they knew something which has endangered them.

One more thing Sir, where is your guard? What was his name... Rehman?? Amir thought for a while... He has left his job, a month ago. I am Sorry, Officer, if I am not wrong, it's the same time when Nancy went missing. What rubbish is this? What are you exactly trying to tell? Sir, that man is an impressionist; he worked as a worker in Edumed Company. So, now you are saying the police department is involved in this? No, Sir... I am just telling you that your wife and Nancy both can be in danger. Please save them as soon as possible. You can't tell me what I should do... You go now; I thought you have something important to tell, but you came here only to divert my mind from you... Do remember, my eyes are always on you... Sorry, Sir, if you will keep your eyes on me then the real culprit will escape. You go now.

Sameer left the police station disappointed. Amir picked up the egg-shaped paperweight and was rotating it continuously. Is it possible that Rehman was a con man and he kidnapped Nancy and then Sara? No. It can't be possible. Where is Sara then? He got up from his chair and went out when a man came into the police station and spoke something to the constable. Amir went to that constable and enquired about that man. Sir, he is an informer; he was telling us about a suspicious couple, who rarely come out of the house. So, I told him what is so suspicious about this, they might have been newly married; he started laughing. Amir gave him a grave look... Sorry, Sir. Ok, give me the address... I have nothing to do, today. I will inspect it myself. Sir, don't go alone; they might be armed. I am just checking, don't worry... If I find anything suspicious, I will call you.

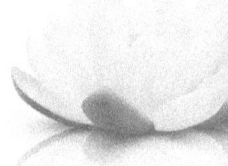

Chapter 35

Nancy was sleeping when she heard a strong crash sound; she woke up and ran directly to Ravi's room, who was already awake and was watching from the window. Nancy whispered, what happened? I think someone is outside. You go and hide; I will see who they are. Suddenly, someone knocked on the door. Open the door... it's the police. He was taken aback; how did they know my location? Nancy told him, it's police, and we can't hide anymore... Go and open the door... No, Nancy, we can't... You go and hide... It's of no use, now... He agreed and opened the door. Officer Amir was standing there with his gun aimed towards the door... He was shocked to see him... Rehman... What the hell are you doing here? Nothing; it's my grandparents' house. By the way, what are you doing here and why are you aiming your gun towards me? Don't play these silly games, now... Where is Sara?

He looked confused... Who is Sara?... My wife?... How am I supposed to know where is your wife?

Nancy who was hiding behind the cupboard came forward...What happened to Sara?... Officer Amir was astonished to see Nancy. So, you kidnapped Nancy?... No, I didn't kidnap her... No, Amir, he didn't kidnap me, I came with him myself. Oh, wow….! The Police are looking for you, and you are enjoying your vacation with him. When I got the tip, I didn't believe it at first, so I thought to check it myself. I came alone, but I am going to call my team and get you both arrested. Amir, please understand; it's not what you think it is. I came with him because my life was in danger. Who do you think is after you? Just tell me where is my wife? Please Amir, try to understand, we are hiding ourselves and don't know anything about Sara. Why exactly are you hiding, and for God's Sake please tell me. Who is after you? And, you Mr. Rehman, you resigned from your post one month ago. I resigned? Who told you so? I confirmed it with the police department. No, no, it can't be so. I was on a department's mission. What do you mean by it? Amir raised his pistol and aimed at Ravi. I am going to shoot you now. Either you tell me the truth or be ready to die. Stop please, Amir. I will tell you everything, but please keep that gun down. I am not your enemy; I am also a victim of all this crap. Nancy interrupted; Amir, please keep your gun down and listen to us. Amir sat on a chair, holding his pistol. Ravi explained to him what all happened to them; Nancy was standing in the room facing the window. Amir stood up from his chair. Nice try, but do you think I am fool? You were working in the Edumed and you are their secret agent. No, I was definitely a secret agent but not of Edumed; I am a secret agent of the Narcotics Department. My senior installed a GPS tracker in my teeth and said it contained information. Amir, I think, my senior, Officer Dhami is the one behind all this, she told me to hide Nancy as her life was in danger, and now, you are telling me that they have dismissed me from my duty. All this was a plan. I am not able to understand what you are saying; even if Officer Dhami is involved in all this, but what will she get from hiding Nancy and tracking you? That's what we need to find out. Amir, maybe your wife knew something, which Officer Dhami came to know about and that's why she has abducted her. We don't know, but the only way to know is through Officer Dhami. Amir, you have to find out. I don't want to show her that I know about my GPS tracker, as I have given it to my friend in the same village and, she might be thinking, it's still with me. Amir, you go to her and try to find something; any clue, maybe her phone, laptop or anything through which we could at least get a clue. Please take my new number and contact me, if you found anything suspicious. Amir was still discontented, I still don't believe you, but I will do it for my wife. He took the chit on which Ravi had written his number and left.

Chapter 36

Police Headquarters, Srinagar. Good morning, Sir. A very good morning, Officer Amir; come in and have a seat. So, how is it going in Pattan? Sir, everything is good. Sir, I want to go to Delhi. Why? In the case of Mr. Faheem's murder, who was killed last month; he had some Delhi connections. I think I should go there and work with Delhi Police Narcotics Department as their company Edumed is notorious for drugs. You are no longer posted in Dal gate station. This case doesn't come under your jurisdiction. Sir, please, I have got a tip from an informer. No, I can't allow you. Sir, an informer from Pattan told me that drug peddlers get supplies from Edumed. It can also be a possibility that Faheem denied working illegally and they got him killed. This is not just a normal murder; it has its roots in Pattan also. Ok, I cannot allow you on the Faheem murder case, but to investigate the drug connections. Do you need your team to go with you? No, sir, I think I will go alone and gather information, involving more people will not be a good idea. Sure, I will make the necessary arrangements for you and will mail Delhi Police about your arrival. Thank you so much, sir. Now go and show me the results.

The next morning, Amir reached Delhi International Airport. He was received by Delhi Police Officers, who took him directly to the headquarters. He was sent into Officer Dhami's Cabin. Hello, Officer Amir, please, have a seat. So, tell me how can I help you? I mean, is there anything I could do for you? Are you working on Faheem's murder case? No, mam, I am just here to check if any drug scandal is involved in his killing. I think he was working for someone in Delhi. I have a tip that he might be a drug dealer and it could be a possibility that he could be working for… Working for who Officer? Working for Black Earth. Amir wanted to see the expressions of Officer Dhami. She smiled a very cunning smile. Ok, then all the best, and do tell me if you could find anything. He stood up and left. He sat in the cabin which was assigned to him and started working on his laptop. After a few hours, Officer Dhami left in the police car for patrolling. This is the right time; I should go and check her cabin. He saw a guard standing outside her room. Hello, my name is Officer Amir, and I might be of some help to you. The guard looked unaffected. He held 500 rupees note in his hand and tried to put it in the guard's pocket. he took it off and gave it back to Amir. He thought I will have to raise the sum; this man will definitely help me if I would increase the money. He could have created a scene if he wasn't interested. He took off 2000 rupees note in his hand and put it in the guard's pocket. Guard smiled and asked, what exactly do you want? I want to go inside Officer Dhami's cabin and you will take care of it so that no one comes inside. Guard smiled and said, for 2000 bucks, I can guard only for fifteen minutes. You can go inside and come within fifteen minutes. If anybody comes, I will knock on the door two times, and then you need to hide. Ok, done, Amir exclaimed and went inside her Office. He opened the drawers, but couldn't find anything relevant. He took the laptop, and tried to open it, but it was locked. He kept it on the table again. He looked in the dustbin and saw some papers and on one paper, he saw his wife's name and number written, which was carefully scribed and the paper was thrown in the dustbin; he took the paper and came out. You took almost twenty minutes, Amir looked towards the Guard, but I need her laptop, I will pay you 5000 rupees, get me her laptop. Do you think I am mad? I can't risk my life for a mere sum of 5000 rupees, but if you can increase the amount of money, I could think about it. Ten thousand? He nodded in disagreement. Listen, I don't have much time; you tell me yourself what amount you need. I want 50000 rupees. Amir looked towards him, are you in your senses? I just need her laptop for an hour and you are charging me a huge amount for it. Guard thought for a moment and then said, Ok 30000 rupees, nothing less than this. I will give you the laptop in the evening and you have the whole night to deal with it, but it should reach me in the early hours before dawn, Amir agreed. Ok, then, let me think what I can do. Now, you go; don't stand here and interact with me, it will be suspicious.

Amir went to the police station and told the officer that he needed to go to Karol Bagh Police station for gathering some information and he would be back in the afternoon and left.

Chapter 37

Amir went to the narcotics department in the evening and saw the guard standing outside Officer Dhami's cabin. He sat in his assigned chair. After a few minutes, Officer Dhami called Amir to her cabin. He got anxious. Why is she calling me? Did this guard told her everything? But I have to go; let's face it. He went inside. Oh, come Officer, please have a seat, you look very tired and troubled. Is everything alright? Yes, Mam everything is alright, actually, Delhi is too hot to handle for me. She laughed and said, yes, it is hot in comparison to Kashmir. So Mr. Amir, tell me about your today's work report, did you find any lead in your wife's missing case? No Mam, not yet, he said without thinking, then he realized he hasn't told her or anybody except Sameer, Nancy and Ravi about Sara's missing case. His eyes spoke millions of unsaid things as he looked towards Dhami in astonishment. Don't be surprised, Mr. Amir, I am a police officer, and I know exactly, why you are here. I think it will be better if you will inform the police and take proper help from them, instead of being a detective by yourself. You might land in a trouble and maybe your wife will also be in a problem. How do you know about my wife? I never told you. Definitely, you didn't tell me, but I do have informers. The way, you landed in Delhi made me think about it, so I dug deep and found out that you think your wife is in Delhi. No, I don't think so. Then tell me why you are here. I am here to do my duty, nothing to do with my wife. She is missing for a few days, and you are doing nothing; coming here to do your duty. You haven't even reported to the police station. Why are you hiding this? Are you involved in your wife's missing case? No, my wife is at her mother's place; she will come back. Don't worry. I hope so, otherwise, you will be in trouble, Mr. Amir, for hiding information and making cover-up stories. She stood up. So, I am leaving; hope you will do what is right and will head back to your state. As soon as she left, the guard came inside to pick up her belongings. He gave the laptop to Amir and left taking everything else. Amir heard the car engine, picked up the laptop and left. He went straight to Karol Bagh to a laptop repair shop and told the person to open it. It took him half an hour to unlock it, and then he handed it over to him. He took the laptop and went to his hotel room. He sat on the chair and drank a glass of water. He could feel his trembling legs and shaking hands while he was opening it. How did she know about Sara? She definitely knew where my Sara is. Hope so, I will get any information from this laptop. He opened the folders, but everything appeared normal, extremely normal. He was about to close it, when he thought I haven't checked C drive, which is mostly kept for storing computer data. He opened it and saw many folders. He opened one folder and saw Nancy's video; it looked as if a camera was attached to Ravi. He was shocked to see his own video, where he was seen talking to Nancy and Ravi. She knew why I was here and that I will be spying on her, then why did she let me in? She could have been more cautious. I think we all are in grave danger; she is much more dangerous than I thought. I should tell Nancy about all this. He called Ravi's new number. It rang and he picked up, as soon as he said hello, He interrupted, don't say my name. There is a camera installed in your flesh or your clothes, I don't know, but it is on you, I saw my video and all the videos in which you and Nancy are talking about the Black Earth. She is keeping her eye on you. Do something, keep Nancy away from you. She knows everything you talk about. She knows all your plans, just don't react, end the call and send Nancy to a safer place. As soon as he ended the call, his phone rang; it was Officer Dhami's call. How was your date with my laptop? Hope you enjoyed it, now let us meet and have a cup of coffee. You have my wife, I know it, please tell me where she is and I will go from here. So, if you want to meet your wife; come to my place and I will make arrangements for you two to meet. I don't trust you. It's your choice, if you want to see your wife, my guard is standing outside your hotel room, come with him, otherwise, you can go back to your state, never to see your wife again. No, don't do anything to my wife, I am coming. He opened the door of the hotel room to find that a guard standing outside his room, Come, Officer, let's go. You knew all this. Come on, Sir, I am a poor man, I need money. Now, don't be the moral police, let's leave. I think you will enjoy it there. Amir left with him. Blue Wagon R car was parked in the parking area of the hotel. Both of them sat and left. The guard looked towards Amir and said... Sir, Mam already knew about you, and she had told me that if you will come to inspect my room or my laptop, I should act as if I allowed you. Where are you taking me? To Officer Dhami's place. Is my wife there? I don't know any of this. I just do what Mam asks me to do. Amir started dialing a number. The guard snatched the mobile from his hand. I almost forgot... but sorry, Sir you are not supposed to contact anyone. Amir closed his eyes… Am I going to get killed, today? Will I be able to save Sara?… Wake up, Sir, we have reached, said the guard.

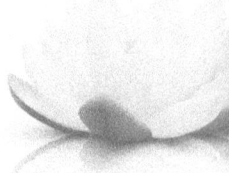

Chapter 38

Amir stepped out of the car and marched towards a beautiful bungalow, entered the gate and moved towards the main door. The guard opened the door from outside and asked Amir to wait in the lobby. Would you like to have something cold or hot? said a voice from behind; Amir turned to see Dhami standing behind him. Amir got up from his chair. Oh, please be seated, what would you like to have? I just want my wife. Please tell me where she is. Don't worry, your wife is safe. I beg you please tell me where she is. So, do you want to meet her? Yes. Ok, I will for sure make you meet her, but you need to do a little favor for me. I will do anything what you say, but please tell me where she is. That's a good deal. You have to bring Ravi and Nancy here. Amir was startled, why do you want to involve those two innocent people? Well, those two innocent people have made things difficult for me. I want two of them to stay away from me and my business. Your business??? Amir just realized something and he could feel sweat flowing down his face. Are you black earth? She smiled. Well, I don't owe you any answer or explanation. Just tell me, if you are ready or not. Amir thought, let me first get Sara out of this s**t, then I will file a complaint against Dhami. What are you thinking, Mr. Amir? You don't have any option, and yes, one more thing, don't you think you could double-cross me. First, you will bring those two here, and then I will free your wife. No, you first hand over Sara to me, and then I will get them here. How am I supposed to believe that my wife is with you? OK, Sure I will let you see her, but you can only take her home after you complete your task... Is that clear? Amir instantly said yes, so that he could see his wife. You wait here only, I will come. Amir could feel his heart beating fast. After ten minutes, Dhami returned with another woman whose mouth was covered with cloth, and hands tied to the back. Sara's eyes lit with happiness upon seeing Amir. Amir jumped from his chair to hug Sara, but Dhami pointed her pistol at the head of Sara, get back this instant or I will kill her. Amir raised his hands and got back; please don't do anything to her, he said with teary eyes. Now, you saw her, you can go now and when you bring them here, you could take her. Amir started to leave. One more thing, Mr. Amir, don't try to act smart, otherwise, it will only take a fraction of second to press the trigger. I hope you understand. No, you don't harm Sara, I will do as you said.

Amir boarded a flight to home. He reached home and was welcomed by his parents and children. Amir, you look tired, sit my child; I will get you some water. He drank water, and everyone was looking towards Amir's face in hope, but Amir just hung his head in despair and went inside his room. He called Ravi and told him everything. Ravi, I don't know what she is going to do to you, and most important, I don't know whom to trust and whom not to. If I will not take you two there, she will kill my wife. Ravi, I hope you might have taken Nancy to the safe place. I don't know what to do. Ravi listened to everything very calmly and ended the call, as he knew Dhami was keeping an eye on him. Amir was so tired that he slept on the couch. He was awakened by his mother. What happened, Mom? Amir, someone is waiting downstairs for you and he is saying he has some important work with you. Amir got up from the couch stretching his body and rubbing his eyes. He went downstairs and saw Sameer waiting for him in the lobby. What on earth is he doing here? Is he also a pawn of Dhami? What are you doing here? Sir, I am here to give you some information? What kind of information? Sir, if you don't mind, can we please sit and talk? Okay, have a seat. Sir, I have a message for you from Ravi and Nancy. Amir was surprised to hear their name. They are ready to go with you. Amir was confused; don't they know how dangerous it could be? I can't risk their lives. Sir, Ravi wants to end this now. What about Nancy? She also wants to go. No, I can't be so selfish, I can't let them die and walk out with my wife. Don't worry, Sir, nothing will happen, you just get ready, we will be leaving by tomorrow and these are your air tickets. Meet them at the airport. That night Amir didn't sleep at all; it was like they were offering a sacrifice, but why? He kept juggling whole night. He left early morning to the airport, there he met both of them and they boarded on the plane; nobody uttered a word, maybe they knew that Dhami was keeping an eye or maybe there was nothing left to talk about now and everybody just wanted to end it for once and all.

Chapter 39

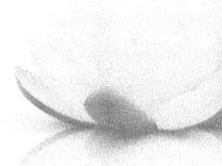

Within forty-five minutes, they landed at Delhi International Airport. They started moving towards the parking lot when an elderly woman approached Nancy. You look so beautiful. Can I hug you? She hugged her and left. Everyone was bewildered. A man holding a placard of Amir's name was standing, they went with that man and upon reaching a deserted place. The car stopped and the driver asked them to get off. They looked puzzled. What are we going to do in the middle of the road? I am just doing what I am told to do so, the man replied. All the three of them got off the car and stood by the side of the road, not sure what to do and where to go. They heard a voice… Come after me. A man in his mid-forties asked them to follow him. They followed him, until they reached a deserted house in the middle of the jungle; it appeared as if this was the house where all the bad things happened. Amir felt guilty for allowing them to come with him. I can never forgive myself, if anything bad happened to them. He tried to pull Ravi's shirt as if trying to stop him, but he looked directly into Amir's eyes affirming that everything is Ok. The man guided them into the house and asked them to wait. The house was more terrifying from the inside; it was so dark and windows were covered with dark curtains, very dim light was there. In the corner, one big table was there and five chairs, randomly scattered in the room. After a few minutes, Dhami came and asked them to pick chairs and sit on them. I am extremely sorry for your inconvenience, but my dear guests, please help yourselves and pick up the chairs and sit. It is so lovely to see my lovely junior over here. You did a good job Ravi, but only problem was that you got too much deep. Ravi smirked, I should have never worked with you, but I need one answer from you, why did you put the tracker in my mouth? Why did you want to track me? Dhami laughed before answering, Sometimes, I doubt, you are my agent! Well, I did this because, you were the one who was working to find out about Black Earth and Edumed, so I need to keep an eye on you so that if someday, you found out about me, I could neutralize you. As you are champion in masking, so I could easily find and kill you. It is so simple, but I am impressed that you found out. Where have you installed camera in my body…? Oh, no, I haven't... Ok... Amir must have told you about that video, I installed that the camera not in your body, but at your grandparents' house. I knew you will go there one day or another, so I installed it there. It was nice to hear about your stories, the way you were speculating, but I must say, you both have a good guessing power. Do you have any more questions or should we proceed to next step? Amir stood up from his chair, where is my wife? Oh, Amir, I am now bored of your repeated question, Anyone else? Nancy, I think you too deserve answers. So darling, you were a scapegoat just like your husband, I wanted to shift the whole focus from me to you, and most importantly, don't you dare to think that Daniel left you all alone; actually, he never went to US. He is also with me along with his brother. Nancy was shocked to hear that. No, you are lying, I am not darling. How could I let him go? He will be the ladder for my promotion. Headlines will be... Officer Dhami cracked the Black Earth mystery... Two foreigners, with one Narco department undercover agent were arrested by Officer Dhami. Just think how the media and masses will applaud me for saving the city. So, Nancy, you will be portrayed as Black Earth. Ravi as a traitor, who worked for you and Daniel, who is already infamous, will help to put a permanent stamp on you being the culprit and no more missions will be undertaken, and then, I can work freely without any stress of getting caught.

Now, nobody will believe you to be innocent as you kept running from the police along with Ravi. It's not so easy being a villain, you see… I work so hard… and started laughing. I think now, all the doubts have been cleared and now, you can take your wife home as promised, she shouted, bring her here. Amir if you ever opened your mouth, I will kill you. Sara was bought inside the room. She went running to Amir and started crying, please take me away from her; they tortured me so much. I want to go back home; please take me home. Nancy looked towards Sara, take care, Sara… Sara went to hug Nancy. As she hugged her, Nancy placed her little Nirbheek revolver on her back and took her to the front. What are you doing, Nancy shouted Amir? Leave her; don't harm her. Move back everybody, or I am going to shoot her and literally believe me I am going to do it. You all have already made my life miserable; now, it doesn't matter if I end up in jail. Ravi joined Nancy and told Dhami to get back. Dhami replied, what do you both think you are doing? If you want to kill her, go on, why will I worry? Nancy smirked and said… Oh, really! You won't be worried? Stop acting, we know everything. So, my dear best friend Sara, would you like to tell everyone the truth or do you like me to do honors? Amir shouted… I was a fool that I trusted you two; I thought you were my friends. Amir, shut up, and sit down quietly, or I will kill her, said Nancy agitatedly. Sara, I am warning you to tell us the truth or get ready to die. Nancy poked her with the revolver. Sara smiled, every day, I was preparing for this day. I knew one day I have to come out, so here is it. Good. Go on and speak, said Ravi. It was all my plan; I did everything. What are you saying, Sara? Dhami tried to reach her phone. Ravi held her hand. Give your phone to me. Dhami handed it over to him. Come on, Sara, we don't have the whole day for it. Start speaking, now. Ok, fine I did it all, I am behind all this and I am Black Earth. Amir felt as if his whole world has crashed. His brain was unable to process what his ears were hearing. Why did you do all this, said Amir with teary eyes? Sara looked into Amir's eyes…You made me to do this! Amir now got frustrated Are you out of your senses? I made you to do this? Yes, said Sara with no remorse. I was a doctor, Amir, and what have you made me? I did everything possible in my hands, but nothing changed. Nobody looked upon me as human; you all thought I was a robot, just to serve you. It used to kill me when I had to ask money from you for every petty thing. It killed me, my self-worth. My self-confidence shattered. So, instead of quarrelling with you and your mother, I skipped reality and made my own world, and where I was the boss. I did what I was good at. I started blogging about medicinal herbs, I never expected any response, but people started messaging me, and they sent me many queries. I started an online website named Edumed selling those herbs. Initially, a very few people purchased from me, but slowly, my profits increased, and I made a huge money, then one day, Officer Dhami contacted me and said she knew about my business, and suggested me sell drugs which were recovered from the Narcotics department. After some time, we started selling addictive herbs. We collected opium and supplied it to the market. In order to conceal our true purpose, we collected other herbs also. I made her my partner as I wasn't able to do it all alone by myself, and then we appointed the MD of our company, who totally had no idea what was going on. After huge profits, we wanted our business to spread to the world, so we appointed foreigners, and our first employee was Gabriel, a very dedicated and shy guy, but he was very witty, it didn't take him too long to know what all is going on here, so we had no other option then to tie him and make him a druggie, we even tattooed his body, so that even if he would escape and go to the police, they will also think of him as a drug addict. When everything was going well, his brother Daniel came looking for him, he worked very hard to find about him. He even worked as a laborer in Edumed. We got him arrested many times so that he will be deported, but he was too adamant, he wanted to find out his brother and expose us, but when he was too close to reach us, Nancy joined in here, and when he got to know, he became worried for her and his focus shifted from exposing us to saving her, but Nancy wanted to go deep, so I had to handle it myself. I became your friend so that I will know about your moves. When you were walking on the boulevard, I saw you and sat in the park, and you came directly to me and then it was very easy for me to do friendship with you. I never wanted to hurt you. I genuinely considered you as my friend, but my business was more important to me than you. You also like your husband who was so eager to know everything, so I had to kill that innocent Faheem because that was the easiest way to get rid of you. I always knew where you were as there was a tracker in Ravi's tooth, we didn't want to kill you, we wanted to use you both. When Ravi took you with him, Dhami told me to go underground leaving my phone there with clues pointing towards Sameer, but my dear husband, you ruined it all, by not complaining to the police. We thought you will arrest Sameer, and then we will attack Nancy and Ravi. Then, we will portray them as masterminds and Sameer as their pawn who works for them, but here again, Amir was only concerned about his honor, so he never complained. I told Dhami to blackmail Amir to bring them here so that she could arrest them in charge of my abduction. We will now portray them as if they were running from police and they kidnapped police officer's wife to use her in exchange for their freedom. Where are Daniel and Gabriel? With the help of Dhami, we got Gabriel out of the police custody as he was getting normal day by day, and we told everybody that they are being sent to their home country, but instead we kept them at our place. Where have you kept them, shouted Nancy. We locked them up in an abandoned house in Uttar Pradesh and kept our one man for their surveillance… but… But, what yelled Nancy? One day, they both tried to run but were caught and… Gabriel got killed, we dumped his body behind that house and from that day onwards Daniel stopped eating, most probably he will also die of starvation. Nancy felt a wave of terror across her body, you killed Gabriel!!! Nancy was barely able to keep her self-standing. Amir was so sad to hear all this. Sara, do you just realize what you did? You became a drug mafia; you could have just joined your job again. I would have always supported you. Now, you are happy after earning so much? Do you think this money has any value? You didn't even once think about me or the kids? What would happen when they will learn that their mother is a criminal? I would make sure that you will get the punishment you deserve. Everybody, freeze… said a strong voice from behind; it was a police officer with Sameer and the police team. You played a good hide and seek with us. Shame on you, you forgot that you were a police officer, he said looking towards Dhami, Arrest both of them.

Thank you, Sameer, you made it all work, said Ravi, otherwise, we would not have been able to expose them. I just did what you told me to do and finally, I would be able to know about my brother. Amir was still sitting on the chair expressionless. Nancy went to him... Amir, I know it's very difficult for you, but you have to be strong for your kids and parents. Amir stood up wiping his tears, I have to go and find Daniel before it's too late... She was about to leave when he stopped her, and she turned back... Nancy, how did you exactly know that Sara was culprit, not the victim? Nancy smiled... When God has to reveal the truth, He opens many doors. Do you remember, when you called Ravi regarding camera in his body... He suggested me to leave with anyone I could trust, because he thought I would be in danger if I was with him. So, we contacted Sameer, and he took me to his new restaurant where he works. When I was sitting there, I saw Edward, I thought maybe my mental illness has again started, but then I saw him talking with the waiter and finally, when Sameer came to me, I asked him if he could see him. To which, he said, yes, and I told him that he was Edward. We confronted him and when I threatened him that I would go to the police, he confessed that he was just an ordinary person working with a construction company. Sara had bribed him to follow me... He just did it for some extra money. But, he realized that it was a big mess when Faheem was killed, but there was no way out, as Sara had threatened him that he would face the same fate as Faheem, if he went against her. Then I realized Sara's plan; she wanted to label me as a mentally unstable person, the same as what she tried to do with Gabriel, but thank God, Edward confessed everything, and we formulated this plan... But why didn't you tell me about all this before, asked Amir?... I knew that you would never trust my words about Sara... The only way, you could trust me was when Sara herself confessed it. So, Ravi told Sameer to meet officer Deepak, who followed us from the Airport. You remember that old woman who hugged me at the airport; she was actually an officer who put this Nirbheek revolver in my pocket. Don't lose strength Amir... You never know how strong you are until time tests you. I never thought I could put someone at gunpoint, but see I did. Thank you, Nancy, you are a brave girl.

Ravi,I am so sorry; I always thought you are the wrong guy, said Nancy.... I was sure you knew something, added Sameer. Thank you, Guys, for saving my job, said Ravi... I had to go now...let me just see what they will confess. He left Sameer and Nancy behind. Let us look for some place to rest; it was quite a hectic day.

Nancy was sitting in the hotel room, she tried to sleep, but couldn't... Thoughts about Daniel haunted her. The doorbell rang... Nancy... Nancy... They have found Daniel and he is in the police station... Come on, let's go and meet him... Nancy could feel her heart bouncing. She ran out of the hotel room and went to the police station. Amir was standing at the main door and escorted them inside. Nancy could not feel herself; it was like a dream for her. She went inside and saw skinny Daniel, sitting on the chair. He saw Nancy; he hugged her and cried like a baby... They killed my brother Nancy... They killed Gabriel... Thank God, you are safe; I thought I had lost you too.

Sameer went to Amir... Sir, did you find anything about my brother Faiz?... Yes, we found out... They were using him as human transport for transporting drugs... But Sameer, he has to face charges as what he did was illegal. Yes, I can understand, said Sameer... But don't worry. I will try to help you legally. Nancy told Sameer............I have something, which I think, should be returned to the real owner. Sameer looked confused... What??? That pheran with white and green motifs that you gave me... It belongs to Faiz's fiancé... Sameer, would you like to do one favor for me? Yes sure.... Then get your brother and Zainab married. What? I can't... She is married to someone else; and, how do you know her name? I know her... When we were hiding, we went to their place. She still misses your brother, and the most important thing, her husband had died... If your brother still loves her and if she agrees to marry a man who has been to jail, then, you must get them married... I will definitely do this.

Amir interrupted them… Nancy, I have talked with the US Embassy; you and Daniel will be returning to your country tomorrow. I have asked the guard of the guest house to parcel your belongings. I am so sorry, Nancy, for all you have gone through. No, you don't need to be sorry… Take care of you and your kids.

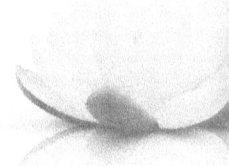

Chapter 40

It was a beautiful Sunday morning; Nancy woke up early went straight to the kitchen and stood by the window holding a cup of coffee. She sat down with her laptop and typed "best playschools for toddlers". Rusty came and started poking the laptop with his snout. Oh, Rusty boy. Go, get the ball, she said throwing Rusty's favorite ball. Daniel came holding their daughter Ellora in his arms. Make a way for the princess, said Daniel smiling. They both kissed baby Ellora. Get ready, Daniel, we are going to visit our first born. Daniel held Nancy's hands; I am so sorry, Nancy. Nancy held his face in her hand and said, Daniel, we both have gone through lot; our baby will always be with us. Let's get ready and go there. They sat in a car and drove to the graveyard where their baby was buried. She kept flowers and silently sat there, Daniel and Ellora also joined her. All three of them held hands and sat silently remembering the baby. They got up then and sat in a car. Car was running on the highway; it was rusty's and Ellora's favorite time. They passed through green meadows and rivers. Suddenly, a flashback of Kashmir just hit Nancy; tears started rolling through her eyes, and she looked towards Daniel and thanked God for saving him. What are you thinking, Nancy? Nothing... I know what you are thinking. By the way, don't you think, there should be a novel written about our lives, Daniel winked....?

Life can be cruel; it can bring us strife.

But we must stay strong and fight for our life.

Thoughts of despair can fill up our head,

We must keep on and move ahead.

Though pain and sorrow come our way,

We must find the courage to face each day,

Though darkness can cloud our view,

We must search for light, no matter how few.

Though we may stumble and fall in the night,

We must find the power to stand tall and fight.

The courage to overcome and accept what's been lost,

We must remember that the future isn't always so dark and so glossed.

We must rise up and be strong,

Look ahead, and not to the past so long,

The future may be uncertain yet we must go on,

Remembering in our hearts that life will soon be reborn.

www.ingramcontent.com/pod-product-compliance
Lightning Source LLC
LaVergne TN
LVHW061545070526
838199LV00077B/6909